BACK COVER

The plan was never to fall in love... The plan was to avenge my father's death.

Hell, I knew better. Never fall in love with the mark.

For ten years I have plotted and planned my revenge against Rafe DeMarco. He took the most important thing in my life away from me and I meant to return the favor.

Except, I was wrong...

Now, I need his protection. And I'm the fool who went and fell in love.

The best laid plans and all.

(Deeper *is the finale of the Deep Duet. Start the duet with Book 1,* Deep.)

DEEPER

M. MALONE
NANA MALONE

MALONE
NANA MALONE

Deeper © January 2018 M. Malone and Nana Malone

MALONE SQUARED

Print ISBN: 978-1-946961-12-9

1

Diana was gone.

Rafe leaned unsteadily against the doorframe to his room, looking out into the empty hallway. When he'd woken alone, he'd gone looking for her. It wasn't until he saw her room that it sank in. The closet was empty, and her purse and shoes were gone.

She'd left him. After everything they'd shared over the past couple of weeks, she'd walked out.

Rafe tried to force the rest of the fog out of his brain. Problem was even though his mind was gaining more clarity, his body certainly wasn't. His legs were still wobbly. And joy of joys, his dick still thought it was party time.

Fuck, why was he still hard? After everything

they'd done last night, his dick should be asleep for a very, very long time.

But oh no, just the thought of Diana and he was ready to go again. Inside his mind, worry warred with self-loathing and rage. Lots and lots of rage.

How stupid was he? He'd let in this woman, whom he didn't know at all, and he'd been had. Where the fuck were his instincts? Someone needed to come and take his assassin card away. Go on and kick his ass out of the club. No more assassin potlucks for him. He'd been played by a novice.

A few months out of undercover work and he was sloppy?

Enough. Think this through.

Who could have sent her? Was this about money? He didn't have any... none that she could access anyway. But the truth was he *did* have enough money to make himself an attractive target for thieves. ORUS had paid him well back in the day. He'd had enough sense to squirrel most of what he'd earned from them into an untouchable offshore account on the off chance that he'd have to run and take Nonna and Lucia with him. He'd made sure they'd never have to want for anything.

But Diana couldn't know about that account, and the only way into it was the account number, both thumbprints, and an eye scan. So this wasn't about that.

And then it hit him. There was something else far more valuable. Fuck, had she stolen the Decker?

He lurched down the hallway, holding on to the walls for balance. Once he reached the kitchen, he paused and forced himself to drink some ice water from the tap and then splashed some on his face. He needed to wake the fuck up. This was definitely more than sex stupor. He'd definitely been drugged. Just what had she given him?

Thanks to the water, his brain was functioning a little more clearly, and his legs were slowly catching up. Now as he lurched, he did so with more purpose. He stumbled into the dining room and then careened around the corner to make sure the Decker was still there.

His heart thumped against his ribs, and his breath came out in sharp, choppy gasps. Oh thank fuck. It was still here.

If this wasn't about stealing the painting, then what was wrong? What could have caused her to do this? Maybe she was scared? His conversation with Noah came back to him in bits and pieces. One of the few reasons a woman lies is because she's afraid.

Rafe frowned. It was possible that Diana was

hiding from something serious. He didn't think it was the boyfriend. Rafe was good at reading people, and he believed the guy when he said he didn't know her. So what was it? He'd told her that he would protect her. He would do anything to keep her safe. She knew that right?

You beat the shit out of that guy? Had that scared her? Had that made her run?

Rafe had done his best to keep that part of him hidden. Sure, he hadn't killed her asshole of an ex, but he'd worked him over good. And he'd enjoyed every second of it. What the hell was wrong with him?

Had she seen the bruises on his knuckles and thought about what those hands could do to her?

But then he thought back to the camera footage. She hadn't been upset. She'd been calm.

He barely made it to the bathroom before he was sick.

To force his body to wake up, he stripped and stepped into the shower. He turned the lever until the water streamed out ice-cold, pelting his skin for as long as he could stand it. After a few minutes of punishment, he turned off the water and toweled off briskly.

He snatched his clothes and headed back to his office. In the midst of his initial shock he hadn't done a thorough search of the safe. He needed to see exactly what she had taken. He was assuming all the cash was gone but he'd had other things in there that were far more valuable.

The thing about intuition was that it wasn't so much there to warn you about awesome things in your life. That little lizard brain in the back of most people's minds usually warned of impending danger or that something was wrong. It was that feeling everyone felt in the pit of their stomach when someone said they needed to talk.

As his hand closed around the doorknob, Rafe had that same exact twinge of intuition, that thing that said, "Hey, dude, shit's about to hit the fan."

And he wasn't ready.

There wasn't much in the safe. Just some files that were better locked away. Files on ORUS agents. Files on undercover work that he'd done. Files he needed to hold on to to keep people safe. There had been cash. Nearly $50,000. All gone. Fine, whatever. He could do without the money.

His eyes immediately did a quick scan for the thumb drive. It was gone. She'd fucking taken it. His stomach dropped.

That friend of his, the intuition, was back.

He looked again, hoping he was just foggy from the drugs. No one went through this much trouble just for money. If so, she'd have taken the Decker weeks ago. No, she'd hung around this long for something more valuable than money. Because the information on that flash drive was worth way more on the open market.

Rafe's head fell forward.

How many people were now in danger because he'd been thinking with his dick?

He didn't have time for this shit. He needed to track Diana down and in a hurry. Still naked, he went straight to his room and grabbed his phone. When he'd bought her phone, he'd connected it to his account.

He immediately pulled up the Find My Phone app. And what do you know? Bingo.

"Gotcha." She was on the move. He squinted, looking at the map. She was near the shopping center where he'd taken her to get her clothes. If he left now, he'd have just enough time to catch her. Maybe. He didn't know what the fuck she was doing, but he was going to get her.

Because after everything, he sure as shit wasn't letting her go.

———

HAD she made the wrong decision?

You don't have time for those kinds of questions.

How had Diana gotten everything so wrong? Her father, her life, her family. Her mind raced, sifting through her childhood memories. Had her father ever cared about her? Had he cared about her mother?

Mama.

Had her mother known? Had she known the kind of man she'd married? Had she brought a daughter into the world, knowing what her husband did to others?

Diana's hands shook as she stepped out of the taxi. Luckily, she hadn't been so shaken that she hadn't remembered to take evasive maneuvers when leaving Rafe's place. She'd walked down the street, crossed over to another street, and then doubled back to the rear corner behind his place before hailing a cab. That way if he had any cameras out front that she didn't know about, he'd think she went east. Not that she'd stump him for very long. But every minute—hell, every second—helped.

She made it to the bargain department store, legs weak and her breath coming out in ragged gasps.

Get it together. You do not have time for this. If you falter, you are a dead woman. Because at the end of the day, Rafe was going to come for her. And he clearly knew how to kill. He might work for the good guys, but she, most decidedly, was *not* one of the good guys. At least her family wasn't. And when he caught her, there was no telling what he would do to her.

You know what you need to do. Stay focused. And get the hell out. When you're safe and out of sight, then you can think this through. But first she needed new clothes, a new bag, and definitely a new phone. And she needed them now. She thought of the rolls of cash in her bag. Rafe's secret stash of money was going to bankroll this little shopping trip. She hated to take money from him, but under the circumstances, she didn't have much choice.

In less than three minutes, she had three sets of new clothes. Jeans, long-sleeved shirts, T-shirts, under-wear, socks. Another pair of shoes. Most importantly, a new phone.

She ran to the checkout line, paid in cash, and then headed straight for the dressing rooms to change. She left the phone Rafe had purchased for her in the bath-room stall. Once he woke up, he'd be able to track her with that. So it had to go.

When all was said and done, she dragged her new clothes into the backpack she'd bought. She tucked her new phone into her back pocket. She snorted softly. The phone Rafe had bought her was a shiny iPhone. The one she'd bought herself was a flip phone. At least it could text though.

Once Rafe tracked her phone—because let's be serious, he would—he'd come here, but he wouldn't be able to find her.

As long as you get out in time.

She hustled herself out of the store, pausing around every corner, well aware of who might be watching, well aware of who might be looking for her. She sent a text to the one person she knew would help her. It was a risk, and she didn't want to put her friend in danger. But right now she needed a safe place to stay for the night. Rafe would be looking for her in hotels.

Diana: Charisse, it's Di. There's been a change of plans. Can I crash?

While she waited, she impatiently inhaled a protein bar, then guzzled a bottle of water. She'd been in such a hurry to leave, she hadn't eaten anything. At least she had the protein bars for now. Once she got to Charisse's, she'd be able to get some real food. She only hoped her friend actually read the message and didn't ignore it since it was coming from an unfamiliar number.

How had she gotten herself into this mess? What the hell was she going to do?

Her first option was to run. Get on a plane, access her trust fund, and bolt. But after everything she'd seen in those files, did she really want to do that? Apparently there were a lot of people, very bad people, looking for anyone named Vandergraff. She could always try going to the man who'd created the fake documents for her, but he worked with her brothers, so that wasn't the safest option.

Which meant that her current identity as Diana Renquist wasn't safe either.

Diana shivered. She had no money, save what she'd taken from Rafe, and her credit cards, which were trackable. What was she going to do?

All she could do was run, use cash, and try to stay off the radar. Maybe color her hair, go back to dark. Go out West. Lay low, live an anonymous life. That was the safest option. But that meant her brothers and Uncle Boris would get away with everything. The things she'd seen in that file... she couldn't live with herself knowing they were involved in human trafficking. They had to be stopped.

Then there was Rafe.

She closed her eyes, caught off guard by the tsunami of emotion that just thinking about him wrought. All this time, she'd been torn by the conflicting feelings she'd had for him. In a way it was vindicating to know that she hadn't been wrong.

Rafael DeMarco was, if not a good guy exactly, at least someone who was working to make the world a better place. An FBI agent. She hadn't seen that one coming.

The text she'd been waiting for came in after a few moments.

Charisse: Of course. You know the address.

With a sigh of relief, Diana called a taxi and then walked to the address she'd given them. She could just download the Uber app or something onto her new phone, but she wasn't taking any risks with her accounts or her emails. Rafe was good. Too good. As it was, he was going to find her soon.

She just needed to have a plan of attack before he did. And maybe, just maybe, she'd get lucky, and he wouldn't find her. She just had to stay ahead of the game.

When her cab showed up, she gave the driver the address and slouched down. She couldn't help but look up at the front of the department store, and then she saw him. Long, lithe movements. Focused drive, and determination in his stride. *Rafe.*

He was already on her tail. Dammit. No doubt, it would take him five minutes to find the phone. Another ten to get security cameras pulled up. Enough to see that she'd walked out maybe five minutes ago, so she had about a fifteen-minute lead before he started calling taxi companies. Fantastic.

She let the taxi drop her off at the library at U Penn. Then she called another taxi, which took her to the residential neighborhoods and dropped her off about five blocks from her friend's house.

She took a back path through a neighbor's yard and then through another. All she could hope for was that none of these houses had motion sensor lights.

When she reached Charisse's house, she walked up to the back door and knocked. Her friend opened the door with wide, surprised eyes. "Hey! What are you doing back here? I expected you to come to the front door."

"Hey. Sorry. It's a long story. Thank you for doing this."

"It's no worry. Richard's on a business trip, and the kids are asleep. They're going to be thrilled to have Auntie Diana here for a bit."

Diana nodded her thanks. "You know I wouldn't do this if I didn't need to."

Charisse frowned. "What are you talking about? You're always welcome. Now, you want to tell me why you're calling me in the middle of the night from a new phone number?"

It was only then that Diana let herself sag, and the

first tears rolled down her face. "Charisse. I'm in so much trouble. And I have no clue what to do."

And then her friend reminded her of why they were so close in the first place. She didn't get angry or say I told you so. Charisse led her to the couch in the living room, put a comforting arm around her shoulders, and said, "Tell me what happened."

un. Run. Run.

Diana jerked awake with a shot of adrenaline in her blood. Immediately she checked her surroundings, looking for the exit. It took her several moments to realize where she was. Charisse's place. She was in the same guest room she'd occupied while she'd formulated her plan for Rafe.

The sheets were soft, and the room smelled like lavender. And the sunlight filtered in through the blinds, casting the room into a warm morning glow.

Diana scrubbed her hands over her face as the events of last night slammed into her like a tidal wave. Forty-eight hours ago, she'd been in Rafe's arms, simultaneously loving being there and hating herself for wanting to be there. That connection she'd felt with him, the one that she'd loathed over the past month, was real. She'd fought it. She'd undermined it. And last night, she'd blown it up for what?

For absolutely nothing, that's what. There was no family to protect. No honor or justice for them. Her family. Her father, her brothers, they were the ones the world needed protecting from. She'd lied, stolen, stalked, and cheated to avenge a man who had essentially sold her off. The bile threatened to rise in her throat again. She dragged in deep breaths to push it down.

Rafe DeMarco, he was one of the good guys, relatively speaking anyway. And to make matters worse, she'd fallen for him. Fallen for his laugh, his smile, fallen for the man that loved his family more than anything in the world. And in the end, she'd hurt him. She'd drugged him, fucked him, and then she'd hurt him. There was something so seriously wrong with her.

She dragged the covers off and after a quick shower, dressed quickly. She found Charisse in the kitchen, making breakfast.

"Morning, sunshine."

Diana gave her a bright smile. "I see you're still a morning person."

"Are you kidding? It's the only time I truly get to myself anymore. I've got two babies under two. I mean, dear Lord. I just finished feeding Jessica, and Braden will be up in an hour demanding something sugary like jam for breakfast, and I'll have to do the mommy song and dance and at least negotiate some toast with that jam as well as fruit. My life is oh-so-fascinating." Her friend cocked her head and studied her. "How are you feeling? A bit better after a good night's sleep?"

Diana nodded. "Thank you. I don't know how to even say that properly. There are no words."

"None are necessary. C'mon. We've been friends forever. So... What's the plan? Besides let your friend make you breakfast and play with your niece and nephew?"

"Honestly, you don't have to make me breakfast. I'm fine. I need to get on the road anyway. Rafe is good. I'm sure I was careless and sloppy somewhere, especially when I started letting my vagina do the talking, so I can't guarantee you'll be safe."

"Stop it. You were running last night. I'm sure you didn't really get that much sleep. I know you won't stay, but at least get something to eat. The least I can do is feed you, because then you'll be out that door and God knows when you'll have a decent meal again. Now sit."

Diana blinked away tears as she listened to her friend. After all, she was right. Last night was probably the most sleep she'd see in a while. Because no one knew she was here, it would be the safest she'd ever be. But she couldn't stay.

If she did, she'd be putting her only friend in danger. Not just her, but her husband, her children.

She already knew the kind of man Rafe was. He wouldn't hurt children. But after what she'd seen about her brothers, she needed to put distance between herself and Charisse. While they didn't know of her entire plan with Rafe, they did know about Charisse. And unlike Rafe, they wouldn't hesitate to hurt the babies if they thought it would get them what they were looking for. And she had a year before she was supposed to marry Uncle Boris.

A shiver ran over her skin. How could they do that to her. Because you don't matter to them. Think of the hundreds of people they've sold. Your only value is in that diamond.

No. She wasn't doing that to her friend. "Thank you."

"So," Charisse asked as she bustled around the kitchen. "What are you thinking the plan is? I'll worry less if I think you at least have one, other than you're going to go in kamikaze style and shoot everyone."

"Well, you can put your mind at ease. No shooting anyone for me. I'm mostly trying the whole stay alive thing right now. I was thinking there might be another way. My father left me a trust. There's one for each of us. If I can get access to theirs, I can maybe send it to the authorities. There's bound to be all kinds of criminal activity." She certainly didn't want any of that money, especially now that she knew where it had come from.

"Are you planning to take that information to Rafe? I thought you were afraid of him."

She sighed. "I'm more afraid of how mad he is at me. I don't think Rafe would hurt me, though he could. He still doesn't know who I am. Right now he thinks I'm just the woman who walked away from him and stole some files."

"And he's FBI. They don't kill people."

Diana hesitated. "Was FBI. Was being the operative word. Now he's Blake Security, and they are a different monster altogether. But for the most part yeah, I don't think they kill people. I've been following them, and not once has anyone they've gone after ended up dead that I can find." She ran a hand through her hair. There was still so much she couldn't tell Charisse. Like the information on ORUS. She had a feeling spilling the beans about a top-secret government organization that trained and used assassins was the kind of information Rafe's so-called friends would certainly kill someone for knowing.

"You said before you were worried about him?"

There was something about the way Charisse asked the question that brought Diana's head up. "I— Yes, I'm worried about him. If my brothers find out what I've been doing this past year or so, they'll go after him. And you, which is why I can't stay."

Charisse narrowed her eyes as she poured pancake batter. "Stop worrying about me. Anything feels hinky, and I'm off to see my sister in Vancouver. Are you sure that's the only reason you're worried about him?"

Diana flushed. "I—"

Charisse laughed. "Honey, it's okay to say you care about him. You said yourself he's a good guy, so it's not a bad thing for you to care about someone."

"It's just I didn't mean to fall for him. And that certainly wasn't part of the plan. A few weeks ago I went into this thing thinking he'd killed my father in cold blood and stolen my mother's jewel. And like a moron, I still let him slide past my defenses and fell in love with him. What kind of a person does that make me?"

Charisse pointed a spatula at her. "That makes you human. It makes you someone who trusts your instincts. It makes you one who believes in the way someone treats you rather than what you've been told."

Diana wiped away a tear. "By that philosophy, I

should have been wary of my brothers all these years. And probably my father. Papa was kind but dismissive, and I always felt like I wasn't good enough. And my brothers, well, let's just say they are not the kind of people I'd use the word love loosely with."

"You're going to have to find a way to forgive yourself, Diana. You didn't know. And they used your ignorance and naïveté against you. You just played right into their hands. Now the question is what are you planning to do with that information?"

Wasn't that the question of the century? It was safer to run. To put distance between herself and Rafe and herself and her family. To take the money she had and hide.

The self-preservation part of her brain wanted to run. Wanted her to just put space between her and the three men looking for her and hide. But she'd spent a lifetime doing that. A lifetime not fighting. A lifetime hiding from her own life. She wasn't doing that anymore. "I can't just leave him. At the very least I can leave information about my brothers' accounts for him. He'll know what to do with it. Though he probably hates me by now and maybe has a shoot-to-kill order on me or something."

"I highly doubt that. Have you stopped to think

that if you were falling for him, then he was falling for you too?"

"Even if that was happening, that's over now. I betrayed him. I lied to him. He introduced me to his family, and they were kind and open. With my running around, they're in jeopardy. He's not going to let that go. Believe me, he's the kind of person that will put his feelings for me aside. If he had any to begin with."

"I don't know. I think you're selling yourself short. Love is a powerful emotion. Even when you're mad at someone, you still love them."

"I promise you, Rafe doesn't love me." She inhaled deeply. "It doesn't matter though. I know the kind of man he is. I knew the first day he rescued me from the ravine. Who was it that said when someone shows you who they are, believe them?" She shook her head. "Doesn't matter. I'm listening to that. He helped a perfect stranger. Invited me into his house, took care of me, tried to protect me from my fake ex-boyfriend. He's a good person, and I'm not letting him get ambushed. I need to see him one more time. I don't really have a choice; I at least have to warn him. Give him time to get his sister safe. Give him some idea of who might be coming after him."

Everything she said about Rafe was true. But also, what Charisse said was true. She'd fallen for him. And damn, she missed him. She missed his smell and the intense way he watched her. She'd seen that kind of intensity in the way Noah watched Lucia. She'd never thought she'd have that. And then when she'd gotten it, she'd thrown it away for some misguided family loyalty.

It didn't matter though. She knew she had to warn him. Once she did that, she'd go. But she'd never forgive herself if something happened to Rafe.

――――――

EVERYTHING WAS GOING TO SHIT.

And from the looks of it, it wasn't going to get any better for Rafe any fucking time soon. He'd spent the whole damn night looking for Diana. From the time-stamps on the security cameras at the store, he had missed her by just ten minutes.

She had been smart enough to ditch her phone. She had also been smart enough to ditch any and all clothing. Not that he'd even thought to put a tracking device on any of it. He should've stuck one into her shoes. *You're losing your touch, DeMarco.* He needed to fucking find her. If for nothing else than to get that drive back. Because right now with her having that kind of information out there, her life was in danger.

He had a stop to make, and he wasn't looking forward to it. He was in a race against time to save her life, and she didn't even know it. When he saw the flash drive had been moved, his heart had stopped. Of course, his mind had run through the gamut of questions.

Had someone hired her to steal information from him? Did she even know what she had? Now that she'd seen those files, what was she planning on doing with them? Was her plan always to sell it to the highest bidder? Despite what his mind knew, his heart remained hopeful. Like a moron.

There was still a possibility that she'd freaked out. That what happened between them was too fast, too soon, too sudden. That she just needed the space to clear her head. *Oh yeah, and she just needed to break into your safe to get that space?*

Or more upsetting, maybe he terrified her with what he'd done to her ex. *If that guy was even her ex at all?*

Rafe replayed the past few weeks over and over again. The guy he'd beaten to a pulp for her. The idiot had claimed not to know her. Of course Rafe hadn't believed him at the time. Instead, he'd kept hitting him, trying to deliver a message that might not have been his to receive.

Someone had hurt her. He hadn't imagined that. Someone had worked her over. And if not that guy, then who?

He knew he was getting ahead of himself. Allowing himself to believe in his fantasy that what they had was real for even a moment longer was going to get her killed.

The fact that she had a decryption device strong enough to open his safe meant she was far from innocent. She had deliberately come into his home to get access to those files. And if not those files, then something else. Which led to his next question... Who the fuck was she?

He'd already done his due diligence and lifted her prints. He'd run them through the system, but so far nothing had come up. She'd never been arrested. Her name was fake. Whoever had set up that ID for her was good. *Very good.* If he hadn't deliberately told Matthias to dig deeper past the initial layers, he wouldn't have seen that her Social Security number had only come into existence two years ago.

Diana didn't exist. How had she ended up at the bottom of that ravine, and just what the hell was she running from?

When he pulled up to the familiar building, his

stomach curled in on itself. *You don't have to do this.* Yes. He did. And a phone call wasn't going to cut it.

To the rest of the world, the building housed several financial companies. But the majority of the offices were owned by LPA. LPA was also known as ORUS. To everyone in the rest of the world, those guys strolling in and out of the building with their sleek suits were finance guys.

Nope, trained killers. The lot of them. And Rafe was walking straight into their den.

He strolled in the building, his shoes making a clapping noise on the polished marble. He stepped into the glass elevator, squaring his shoulders and preparing for a fight. Because at the end of the day, he might not walk out of here.

When he reached the twenty-eighth floor, the receptionist with her gently graying hair and deceptively unlined face nearly fell over herself as she stood. "Libra?"

Wow, Lila was still here. What had it been? Fifteen years? "Lila. It's good to see you."

She stammered. "B-but, they said you were dead."

Rafe shrugged. "Rumors of my demise have been greatly exaggerated. I'm here to see Phoenix." He shook his head. "I mean Orion. He's expecting me."

Lila nodded and made the call immediately. Rafe

had texted Ian earlier to let him know he was coming in. When he and Noah had performed their coup last year replacing Orion and making Ian the new Orion, Rafe thought he was done with this place. But he would never be done.

In the shakeup of last year, he'd become the unofficial record keeper. When he'd been FBI, he had files on every single ORUS agent. All their kills, personality types, and psychological profiles. He'd stolen that data over the years, though Rafe figured the files had to be heavily redacted. At least compared to the ones the new Orion had allowed him access to.

Noah had made a good choice putting Ian in charge. Ian had managed to drag ORUS back into the right side of the shadows. Ian certainly wasn't pleased about Rafe having the dossiers on all his agents and past missions, but he understood the necessity of their tentative truce. In case any of them ever decided to go rogue again, those files kept everyone alive. They were one hell of an insurance policy. And right now the files were compromised.

One of the men came down to meet Rafe, and he almost had to smile. The kid looked as young as Noah had looked when he started. Barely eighteen, clean-shaven face, good-looking kid. He could probably talk himself into all kinds of places.

When he was led to Ian's office, he found the man in question sitting behind a massive glass desk, staring out the floor-to-ceiling windows. "The power looks good on you, Ian." Ian was just a few years Rafe's senior, but he seemed much older. Like he'd been wielding the power for too long.

He turned slowly with a smile. "Rafe. I wish I could say it was good to see you. But I have to assume you're only here because there's trouble."

They shook hands, clapping each other on the back briefly. "Yeah, I'm afraid so."

Ian nodded. "FBI kind of trouble or people are going to die kind of trouble?"

Rafe shook his head. "People are going to die kind of trouble. I'm here to warn you."

Ian's brows drew down. "You realize we're assassins, right?"

"I know. The team is more than capable of taking care of themselves. But you've got agents at risk. Those files that you refused to have locked in the bureau, the ones you trusted me to hold on to because no one was looking for me. Those files? They're gone."

Ian's face remained completely impassive. But Rafe could see the vibrating anger on Ian's shoulders as they stiffened. "Define *gone*."

And this was the part where Rafe had to swallow

crow. Damn birds could be so tough to swallow when you had to eat them whole. "Spy. That's my best guess. I was infiltrated a few weeks ago. It took that long for them to get access to my safe. I discovered the files were missing yesterday."

"How exposed are we? What is on those files?"

"All the missions before Noah got out. Every agent location, their missions, their strengths, weaknesses, possible leverage. Blood type. DNA. All the new agent information since you took over. You weren't as thorough, obviously. Shall I go on?"

Ian's voice went chilly and icy. "Noah insisted that I entrust you with that information, and now you're fucking telling me it's gone?" He planted his hands on the glass, his anger making the desk shake.

Rafe met his gaze levelly. "Yes. That's my fuckup. It's on me. I'm getting the files back, but in the meantime, you might want to move your agents."

"You're in here telling me how to run my shop? I will run my agents how I see fit. You know we have open ops?"

Rafe didn't appreciate the dressing down, but he deserved it. This shouldn't have happened on his watch. But he'd been thinking with his dick. "I know that. I'm here as a courtesy."

"Some fucking courtesy. How long do we have before that information is sold?"

"There's no chatter on it. No one's made inquiries yet. I'll get the file before it gets that far."

"I think you forget, I'm Orion now. *I'll* get those files."

The fuck he would. Because Rafe knew what that would mean for Diana. "*I'll* get the files. If one of your men goes anywhere near the target, I'll be forced to take them out."

Ian pushed himself to standing. "Are you fucking kidding me right now? You lose the files that compromise all of us, and then you want me to let *you* handle it?"

Rafe rolled his shoulders. "Yes. Because at the end of the day, you don't work for yourself anymore, and I'll remind you again, this is a courtesy call. All active agents should be moved. I will retrieve the files and notify you when it's done. And I'm serious, Ian, keep your men away. I see even one of them, and it's not going to go down pretty."

Ian narrowed his eyes and glowered at him, jaw clenched. "I think you're forgetting my name is Orion now. I answer to the United States government. Not to you."

Rafe nodded. "Fair enough, *Orion*. Like I said, this

is courtesy. And as far as you're concerned right now, with my ties to the FBI, I *am* the United States government. I'm serious, Ian." He said his name deliberately. "You go near the target, it's not going to go well. I will deliver the files to you and guarantee no exposure."

Ian nodded and crossed his arms. "If you don't deliver on that promise, maybe it's time you start watching your back."

3

Back at home, Rafe stared at the clothes and the phone he'd retrieved from that bathroom trash can at the department store the previous night. He examined the items with a sick fascination. Would these be his last memory of her? The things she'd been wearing and using when she left?

It was a depressing thought.

Almost as depressing as realizing just how close he'd been to finding her. The store employee he'd talked to confirmed that he'd seen her only ten minutes prior. There was a chance that she'd been in the store at the same time he was, maybe even close enough to touch.

You know how to hide, don't you?

Well, she'd done better than Rafe had expected.

Perhaps it was arrogance, but when he'd left his place last night, he'd honestly believed he'd be coming back with a reluctant Diana in tow. With his training, it had never occurred to him that she might evade him. Which led him to wonder, just who was Diana Renquist? Because she definitely wasn't the helpless woman in need of rescue she'd led him to believe she was.

"I can't do this," he muttered. His mind was too scattered to focus, but he couldn't allow the trail to go cold. He pulled his phone out and dialed a number from memory.

Rafe waited impatiently as the phone rang. It dimly occurred to him that it was way too early to call anyone, but he didn't give a fuck. Diana was out there in the world doing fuck all, and he had no way to tell if she was safe.

Listen to yourself. If she's safe? You need to be worried about whether she's selling you out right now.

He thrust a hand through his hair, feeling like his heart was going to beat out of his chest. She had no idea what the information she'd taken was worth. Not only that, how much heat it would bring on her. If word got around that there was a woman walking around New York with information on ORUS agents, she might as well have a target on her back.

Which just made his heart pound harder. It was too much, the idea of Diana out there alone where he couldn't protect her. He needed Noah to wake the fuck up. Immediately.

He hung up and called back, letting the phone ring and ring. Finally a sleepy, gruff voice answered.

"Jesus, it took you long enough. Wake up. I need your help."

He could hear rustling and then Noah's voice whispering. A second later, he was back.

"I'm here. What's going on, Rafe?"

"Diana's gone."

A pause. "Gone as in... Wait, did you two have a fight or something?"

Rafe growled. "She drugged me and then got into my safe somehow. I don't know what happened. I didn't have time to review much security footage before I left to track her. She took everything. *Everything*, Noah."

A gasp on the other end let him know that Noah understood how serious the situation was.

"Fuck. Who do you think she's working for?"

"I don't know. But I need to find her before anyone else does. She probably has no idea what she's gotten herself into. You can't just sell this kind of information. Can you imagine what they'll do to her? They won't pay for it; they'll just kill her and take it."

Noah cleared his throat. "Rafe. You know Ian..."

"Don't even say it. I already warned him that I'll fuck him up if he touches one hair on her head."

Quiet. Rafe gritted his teeth. He knew what his friend wasn't saying. Threats wouldn't stop Ian from sending agents after her if they discovered she was actually trying to sell ORUS secrets. Not to mention that he technically should be more worried about getting the information back than saving Diana's skin. It was too confusing to think about in the moment, this strange compulsion he had to protect her, despite the fact that she'd clearly only been using him.

"I need Matthias," he said quietly. It was humbling to ask for help and not the easiest thing to do. He'd been trained to be self-sufficient. Not to need anyone. But right now he'd ask for help from the devil himself if it got him what he needed.

Diana had managed to stay two steps ahead of him so far, but it was doubtful that she could evade someone with Matthias's skill. Plus he had a few things that could help track her. He doubted that she'd remembered to wipe her old phone before she'd ditched it. She was clearly not the helpless innocent he'd assumed, but there was very little chance that she was on his level.

"I'll find you," he muttered.

The question was what would he do with her when he did?

"You know we've got your back. Anything you need, we're on it," Noah vowed. "I don't know what her agenda is, but we'll be ready."

Protectiveness flared. "No one touches her."

Silence. When Noah didn't respond, Rafe's heart rate increased, like he was preparing for a fight. It didn't make any sense, his instinctive urge to protect a woman who'd done nothing but lie and steal from him, but his emotions weren't taking directions from his brain right now. All he knew was that anyone who touched Diana would be on his kill list. The scariest part was he wasn't sure he could check that urge, not even for his nearest and dearest friend.

"Rafe, we don't know what this woman has in store for you. We need to figure out if she's a threat."

"No. One. Touches. Her." Rafe squeezed the phone and then forced out a breath. "I'll take care of Diana. Just get me an address." Then he hung up.

The phone immediately started ringing again, but Rafe ignored it. Instead, he walked into his bedroom and stared at the mussed covers on the bed. Nothing made sense right now, but the only thing he knew was that he couldn't let Diana get away.

Whatever this thing was between them, it wasn't over.

Not by a long shot.

———

DIANA DRIED the last dish and put it away in the cupboard. She turned around and watched as Charisse prepared a bottle for her son, who was currently smashing cheerios on the tray of his high chair. The little boy grinned at her.

"Here you go, baby." Charisse kissed the top of his head as she handed him the bottle and then reached past Diana to pick up the dish towel.

"He's so cute, Char. I almost can't believe how big he is." She sighed. It was one thing to talk to her friend on the phone and hear about her life and another to see it up close. This was real. Real and wonderful and exactly what she'd always hoped she'd have one day. She wouldn't put this beautiful life her friend had created in jeopardy.

As if she could read her thoughts, Charisse squeezed her arm. "You really don't have to go. Stay with us. I'm worried about your being on your own."

Diana pasted on a smile she didn't really feel. "I'm always on my own. That's what I'm used to."

"But you don't have to be. Not anymore. We're here for you, and we have the space." She bit her lip. "Well, we can make the space. It's better than my sitting here freaking out every day wondering what trouble you're getting into."

Diana walked out of the kitchen and down the hall to the spare bedroom she'd been staying in. Her friend had been so accommodating, but she knew Charisse's husband Andrew had to be tired of sharing his office with his wife's old friend from college.

She just had one more thing to do, warn Rafe, then she'd be in the wind. And she'd learned from experience, it was better to go to him than have him come for her.

"I know you've been worried about me. But you don't need to worry anymore. I'm done playing detective. I found way more than I bargained for, and I've learned my lesson. This is what you wanted, right? For me to stop poking my nose into dangerous places? For me to move on with my life?"

Charisse stood in the doorway, watching her as she made up the futon where she'd slept.

"Yes, I wanted you to stop poking around, but you're too far gone now. That's like poking a bear until it wakes up and then deciding the game is over. You've got a monster to deal with now."

Diana sat down on the edge of the futon, the stress of the past few days finally catching up to her all at once.

This was bad. Really bad.

"I wish I'd never opened that safe," she whispered.

"But you did. So what are you going to do about it?" Charisse countered.

"I have no idea." Diana figured she'd better come up with one fast because the kind of information she'd gotten her hands on came attached to some very bad people. People she'd been so sure she could trust.

"Having this information is like putting a target on my back."

"Well, then put it back!" Charisse argued. "Maybe that's all he's waiting on. If he sees that you aren't going to use it, then he shouldn't come after you, right?"

Diana chuckled softly. Then an image of Rafe prowling after her like a big jungle cat made her breath catch in her throat. It wasn't too far off the mark, was it? He was a predator. It was what he'd been trained for. The government wouldn't have used him for all those years if he wasn't great at his job. Clearly he was experienced at tracking down people far more savvy at this espionage thing than she was.

She was so far out of her league.

"I don't think that's going to fix this, Char. People like that don't just forgive and forget."

Charisse sat gingerly on the edge of the bed next to her. "Maybe not, but those people aren't Rafe and Diana. I don't care what you say, there's more going on here. You care about him, and I don't think he'd have taken care of you the way he did if he didn't feel something too."

"I felt something," Diana finally admitted. "But I also lied to him. Plus he now knows that I was planning on drugging him since I had those pills in my purse. Whatever he felt is long gone now, I'm sure."

And damn if that wasn't a depressing thought.

Charisse put an arm around her shoulders and pulled her close. "Well then, just put the information back and then run like hell. You've watched him all these months, surely you know him pretty well by now. Use that. When you see an opening, take it. He's not going to be expecting you to sneak back in, right?"

The more Diana thought about it, the more she liked the idea. Leaving and not coming back was truly her only option. But if she was going into hiding, it would be better if she didn't have to look over her shoulder for Rafe the whole time. It was already going to be difficult evading her brothers. Now that she knew what they'd planned for her with Uncle Boris, she figured they wouldn't take her disappearance in stride. She'd probably spend the rest of her life hiding from them. It would be better if she wasn't trying to hide from Rafe too.

"Okay, I'm going to do it. I'll wait for an opportunity and then sneak back in there. I just hope that's the end of it."

As Charisse hugged her tighter, Diana wished that wasn't a lie. Because even with everything going on, she knew her heart definitely didn't want this to be the end.

The traitorous thing was wishing hard for just one more chance to see Rafe.

———

DIANA PEERED ACROSS THE STREET, her eyes watering with intensity as she scrutinized every person who passed in front of Rafe's building. She was waiting for him to leave so she could sneak back inside and leave the flash drive, along with a note to be careful and watch his back. It was a risky move, for sure, but she couldn't risk leaving it anywhere else.

Maybe you should just erase it.

She bit the edge of her thumb as her mind flashed

through alternatives. It was taking a risk to sneak back into his home and leave it for him. Hadn't she taken enough risks lately? Diana sighed. Everything was so mixed up now, and there was no way to tell who was good, who was bad, and where she fit in. But despite everything, she still felt compelled to protect Rafe. He'd obviously kept these files secret for a reason. Maybe they were his insurance policy against the people he'd worked for. Whatever the reason, she knew he wouldn't have kept them if they weren't important. As illogical as it may be, she didn't want these to fall into the wrong hands.

Erasing it wasn't enough. She didn't have a tech background, but even she knew there were ways to recover information that had been erased. Considering the kind of sensitive information on the drive, the safest place for it was back with Rafe.

Ten minutes later, she stiffened when she saw Rafe's SUV pull out of the underground parking garage. This was what she'd been waiting for. He was on his way to work, so she could go drop this off and then be on her way. It was a scary thought, and Diana shivered. After this, she was on her own. There was no one that she could rely on. No one she could trust. Her only plan for survival was to run. Run! And never look back.

She took the elevator to the top floor and then crossed her fingers that her key would still work. It was her hope that Rafe hadn't been able to get the locks changed so quickly. Another reason she had to move fast and do this now. If she didn't do it now, she'd never have this opportunity again.

When the key slid in easily and turned, she let out an audible sigh of relief.

"Thank God!" Diana pushed the door open and then silenced the alarm. She had to move fast because knowing Rafe, his alarm system would notify him that it had been turned off. But she'd waited ten minutes before going in, so he was already across town. There was no way he could get back here and catch her in the next sixty seconds unless he sprouted wings and flew.

In shock, she looked around the apartment. It was a mess, which was so unlike Rafe. The books on the coffee table had been shoved to the floor, and when she reached the bedroom, her eyes took in the rumpled sheets and the clothes all over the floor. Rafe was usually so meticulous that he couldn't stand to see anything that wasn't in its place. He had a military-like love of order, and it made her sad to see what she'd driven him to.

This is what you've done to him. It's better if you leave and never come back.

Although there was a selfish part of her that wanted to take her chances and confide in Rafe, seeing the tangible evidence of his rage made it clear just how unrealistic that hope was. She'd hurt him and betrayed him. Why would he care about what she had to say? Even if she explained everything and even if he believed her, there was no guarantee that he'd be willing to protect her. Why should he put his life on the line to protect a woman who'd lied to him from the start?

Diana dug in her pocket until her fingers hit the flash drive. She could put it back in the safe, and this would all be over. Just then she heard a noise behind her. Before she could even turn around, she was yanked backward and hit the wall.

"What—" Her scared squeak faded away when she saw Rafe towering over her, his face twisted into a mask of fury.

"You thought it would be that easy?" he growled.

Even as fear filtered through the shock, desire made itself known. Diana whimpered and clenched her thighs together as a tingle of awareness made her core clench. He looked furious, but somehow she knew he wouldn't hurt her. Her knowledge was confirmed when he leaned over her, caging her underneath him, and buried his face in her neck. Diana sighed and angled herself to give him better access. What was it about his touch that made her so hungry for more? Her skin was practically crying out for him, and she'd only been gone two days.

"Do you have any idea how worried I was?" he rasped against her throat in between hot kisses to the bared skin. He began kissing his way up her jawline until he buried his hand in her hair and turned her toward him so he could cover her mouth with his.

Diana didn't fight it, just melted beneath him and allowed him to direct how she moved. Her thighs opened of their own accord, and he moved right in between them like he belonged there. When he settled against her, everything inside her woke up and flared to life. Nothing else mattered but this.

She could fool herself that she'd come back to protect him or to keep the information from falling into the wrong hands, but there was no denying that a part of her had come back because she was drawn to him. Everything inside her wanted to be where Rafe was. Always.

"What are you doing?" she choked out when his hands went to the button on her jeans. She gasped again when he practically ripped the zipper off while pulling it down.

"Reminding you." Rafe yanked his own shirt over his head and dropped it to the ground behind them.

"Of what?"

She gasped as his hand slipped inside her jeans and between her legs, the heat of his fingers branding her as it lit her on fire. Diana let out a harsh groan as those talented fingers rubbed and manipulated the aching flesh that suddenly felt very empty.

"Of whom you belong to. Whom *this* belongs to."

Before she could respond to that arrogant statement, Rafe kissed her again, their tongues tangling wildly as they each fought to take control. Even though she'd always been an aggressive kind of woman, there was just something about Rafe that made everything feminine and soft inside her wake up and melt under his hands. Maybe it was the way he always slid one hand into her hair, like he wanted to hold her everywhere that just did it for her. Diana couldn't pinpoint what it was, but every single time they kissed, she turned into a puddle of mush. This time was no exception. Within minutes, she was whimpering and rubbing against him, desperate for what she knew he could give her.

Despite the internal warning blaring in her mind that this was not a good idea, Diana started pulling frantically at her own clothes, almost breaking a nail in her haste to get her jeans down her legs. Her eyes took in his naked form greedily, trying to soak up all that sexiness just in case she didn't get to see it again. Diana wasn't fooling herself that this was anything other than a goodbye fling.

Even if Rafe didn't know that yet.

Once they were both naked, he didn't waste any time. He lifted her easily in a smooth move that made Diana want to sigh dramatically at the show of strength. But before she could focus on that, all her attention was pulled to where they were plastered together chest to thigh. With nothing between them now, she could feel everything. Every muscle, every twitch of his thigh.

Every twitch of that big, hard thing that was definitely *not* his thigh.

Diana was already getting lost in it, her whole being focused on touching her lips to every inch of the smooth skin presented to her. She ran her hands through his hair, loving the feel of the thick strands gliding through her fingers. As Rafe brought her higher, he bit her throat which caused her to arch her back slightly.

"So beautiful," he whispered. "Don't run away from me again. Need you." He spoke so softly that Diana wasn't sure if he'd intended her to hear that last part.

"I'm sorry. I'm so sorry," she repeated over and over. But instead of making it better, the soft words seemed to make him more frantic. His hands clenched her hips tighter, and his lips sucked at her neck.

"Why can't I stop wanting you? Even when I know you're lying to me, I still can't stay away."

Diana's mind spun at his angry words. He wanted her despite everything she'd done. She experienced an almost dizzying elation at the thought before she shuddered in his arms. It was impossible to hold the train of thought while Rafe was licking her neck and her core was rubbing against his stomach, but she tried anyway. Then she thought of the flash drive.

"Rafe, I wasn't trying to hurt you. I was scared. That's why I ran."

"I know you must be confused by the things you saw. But I would never hurt you, Diana."

Diana clutched him tighter, wishing she could show him that it wasn't about him. She hadn't run away because of the things *he'd* done but because of the things *she'd* done. More than ever, Diana understood what it was like to do bad things for good reasons. She'd come here under false pretenses but only because she'd truly believed that Rafe had stolen her mother's jewel and murdered her father in cold blood. If there was a way to go back in time and tell the Diana of a few months ago that she'd been deceived, that the men in her family weren't the men she'd thought, things would have been different.

Then she cursed herself as a liar because she knew she wouldn't have changed a thing. Even if she could go back, she wouldn't stop herself from coming here because otherwise she would have never known Rafe. She would have never known what it felt like to be cherished.

Then she wasn't thinking at all because Rafe lifted her and slid so deep that her eyes rolled back in her head. Diana screamed from the sheer pleasure, and Rafe paused, those dark eyes she loved, roaming her face to make sure she was okay.

"Too rough?" he whispered.

Her nails tightened in his shoulders, and he hissed at the pain.

Diana tightened her legs around his waist. "Don't you dare stop!"

He grinned before he rocked his hips again, grinding deeper. They both moaned at the sensation, and Rafe's fingers tightened under her ass. Diana clutched him closer, her hands roaming over his muscular back and shoulders as she hung on for dear life. He must have liked that because he growled, a low, sexy sound that instantly made her wetter before he set a frantic pace that had her head banging against the wall.

"Oh my God!"

Diana panted, taking in short, sharp breaths as her desire raced out of control. He was so strong, and the fact that he was holding her while he fucked her against the wall was such a turn-on. She purred as the thought of him controlling her body so easily made her think of the other ways he could take control. She wouldn't have thought she'd ever like the idea of being restrained in any way, but every time he picked her up or held her still so he could do all these dirty, delicious things to her, it was impossible to pretend she didn't respond.

Soon Rafe was grunting in her ear along with every thrust, and she felt the change come over him. He was rapidly losing control, his hips swinging wildly and his lips moving over hers frantically as he got closer. Diana loved it, seeing him lost in his pleasure, and she thrilled at the idea that she could make a man as stoic as Rafe lose his mind like this. She tightened her internal muscles around him, which felt so good that she moaned.

When he moved, he hit that spot that Diana hadn't even known existed until a few weeks ago, and suddenly she was coming, biting and scratching as she wailed against his shoulder.

"Fuck! I can't... Diana, I love you." Rafe squeezed her so tightly that she almost couldn't breathe, and then he shuddered as he came too.

For a long time they rested there against the wall until he pulled back slightly to put her down. When Diana looked down and saw the moisture on her thighs, she realized what they'd forgotten in their haste.

A condom.

"Oh shit."

4

Rafe didn't understand why Diana's expression went from soft and languid to horrified in the space of a second until he looked down. When he saw the moisture on her thighs, he stilled. It took his brain a minute to comprehend what he was looking at since he was still floating on the high of pleasure he could only find in her arms.

"No condom," she whispered.

Rafe would never admit it to her, but for a brief moment he felt a flash of joy. What was that about? He had never been the type of guy to dream of family, a white picket fence and a little woman waiting for him to come home. Considering his line of work, that was wise. Because having a family that loved you was just one more point of weakness, something your enemies could exploit.

But there was no denying that the idea of Diana getting pregnant and carrying his baby sent a rush of masculine appreciation through him. Shaking off the crazy thoughts, Rafe ran a hand through his hair as he considered how to handle the situation. This had never happened before, which was telling in itself. After this many years, reaching for a condom was an ingrained part of sex.

"I'm sorry. I don't know what to say. I've never forgotten a condom before."

Her eyes flashed to his at the revealing information, and Rafe turned away, not ready to have her examine him that closely. They hadn't settled anything between them yet. Why had she run, and what was she doing sneaking back into his place? Luckily, he'd expected her to try something like this, so he'd started circling the block for a while every time he left home, giving him time to get back home as soon as the alarm alerted him. But just because she'd come back didn't mean he trusted her.

And obviously Diana wasn't planning on trusting him anytime soon since she looked like the possibility of having his baby was a fate worse than death. The thought stabbed at his heart a little, but he could hardly blame her. What did she know of him really? That he had a shady past and couldn't tell her anything real? Not exactly prime husband material that women dreamed about.

"It's okay. I'm on the pill. I was just surprised."

Rafe tipped her chin up so she couldn't avoid his eyes. "I was, too. I've never been irresponsible before. You make me lose control in a way that I've never experienced."

Her breathing increased slightly before her eyes shuttered. "Let me just clean up." She walked into the bathroom and shut the door. A few seconds later, he heard the water come on.

Rafe had taken two steps after her before he caught himself. How pathetic that it made him nervous to have her out of his sight even for the few minutes it would take her to rinse off. There was no window in the bathroom, so she couldn't escape. And even if there was, they were too high up for that to be an issue.

By the time she'd finished showering, Rafe had his clothes back on and was sitting on the bed, gun at the ready. He wasn't accepting lies from her. And while his dick couldn't stay away from her, his mind was in control now. He didn't want to give her time to think up lies.

She stopped short when she saw the gun.

"Who sent you?"

The question—and the gun—took her off guard,

he could tell. What had she expected? Did she really think that she could walk back in here and he wouldn't have any questions for her? If she did, she clearly hadn't done that much research on him. Anyone who'd come into contact with him in the past knew that he was relentless when it came to getting the information he wanted. He'd killed for it before.

"None of that matters anymore. All you need to know is that I came here to find a rare diamond called the Jewel of—"

"Of the Sea. That blue diamond," Rafe finished, his jaw tight. This whole thing was about that stupid diamond? He'd brushed it off when Alan had mentioned it before, but now he wished he'd paid closer attention. He'd just been annoyed at the implication that he'd stolen it, but apparently his superiors at the FBI weren't the only ones who suspected it had been taken. If others believed it enough to send a female spy to honey trap him into revealing the location, that was bad.

Really fucking bad.

Diana's eyes narrowed. "Yes. As soon as I found out that you were the one who stole it years ago, I knew I had to try to get it back. But I failed, so... end of story."

Rafe's mouth fell open. Of all the things he'd expected to hear, that was at the bottom of the list. Of all the many things that he'd done, he'd never been a thief. But if he had taken it, it would take an army to get it away from him. Not one lone woman who looked like she'd scream if she saw a spider.

Diana had actually thought she could come here and steal the diamond back?

He gave a low harsh chuckle. He'd assumed she'd just been sent in to find the location and report back to someone else. Not that she'd ever try to actually take it herself.

"Stop laughing at me, you asshole!"

His laughter cut off when she hurled herself at him. But she didn't come at him with flapping hands and an uncoordinated attack, she came at him with elbows and fists and... rage.

What the fuck? What happened to the damsel in distress? She landed a sweeping elbow across his cheek, and he cursed low. She quickly followed it up with a punch aimed right for his nose. That one he deflected.

Someone had taught his delicate flower how to fight. And how to fight well. He mostly deflected her blows, refusing to land any of his own. But he quickly realized all that was getting him was beat to shit.

With a growl, Rafe flipped them over and grabbed her hands between one of his. Controlling her easily, he waited until her thrashing calmed down. Then his heart clutched when he saw the tears on her cheeks.

"Fuck, Di. Why are you crying?"

The nickname only seemed to enrage her. She screeched and tried to buck him off, but he was too heavy. "Because I know you know where it is, you asshole. None of this was supposed to happen. I wasn't supposed to feel like this. When I left, I knew you didn't have it, but now you obviously know all about it. You *have* to know where it is."

"I don't know anything about it."

She scoffed. "Yeah right. All sources indicate it was there before you paid Dieter Vandergraff a visit. Yeah, I know about that too. Your flash drive was very informative. Although I already knew about what you do. Who you are."

Rafe tried to cover his shock. How was that possible? Then he thought about his little visit to Ian. While the reins of power had shifted at ORUS recently, prior to that, there was no doubt that Orion would have loved to see his downfall. Even though Rafe DeMarco was officially dead, there was always the possibility that Orion had sold information about him, hoping to smoke him out of hiding. Faking his death had worked on everyone else, but it would be completely within character for the former Orion to have had doubts.

"So you betrayed me for money? Was it worth it, sweetheart?"

Diana's eyes went white hot. "*I* betrayed *you*? Hah! And it wasn't about the money."

She tried to buck him again, and he firmly planted his hips on hers to keep her from moving. But shit, that sent his blood pressure soaring. "What was it about then?"

She seemed to be considering her answer. Then she shook her head, and he knew he'd lost her. She wasn't ready to trust him yet. "Nothing. This is just a job to me. No more, no less."

Rafe didn't believe that for a second. But until she decided to trust him, he had to accept it.

"Whoever sent you on a job like this should be shot. This isn't safe. You shouldn't be approaching dangerous men on your own. What if it had been someone other than me? Anyone else would have hurt you, Diana."

He hated to think what could have happened if she'd pulled this shit on any of the other ORUS operatives.

"It doesn't matter anymore because I've failed. I have no clue what will happen to me now."

She looked so miserable that Rafe couldn't resist a soft kiss to her forehead. He would keep her close.

Eventually she would give up her secrets, and he'd figure out who sent her. It was the only way he could keep her safe.

"Don't worry about any of that now. You're safe, and you're going to stay that way."

She narrowed her eyes at him. "You can't make that promise. No one can. I've gotten myself in deeper than I ever imagined. There's no going back now. All I can do is disappear."

The thought of her leaving him again, of her being out of his reach, sent a bolt of pure fear through Rafe. Never mind the fact that he could track a whisper on the wind, there was no way she could successfully hide from him for long, but just the idea that she might try made him want to keep her chained to the bed.

Fuck. Control, asshole.

He had to control those base urges. She already thought he was a monster, clearly. He'd watched her face when she mentioned what he'd done to Dieter Vandergraff, and she'd looked disgusted.

As she should be, he thought morosely. *It's in her best interest to see you as you truly are. Dangerous.*

He loosened his grip on her wrists slightly. "I'm going to let you up now. Don't try anything."

Although her eyes narrowed reflexively at the order, she didn't try to pull away from him. When he released her hands, she lowered her arms slowly and flexed her fingers.

"What now? You can't change my mind, Rafe. I know what I'm doing."

Rafe moved back and allowed her to slide off the bed. "Do you? Because I sure as hell don't."

———

DI RUBBED HER WRISTS ABSENTLY, pretending that she wasn't ogling Rafe as he moved around the room. Finally she gave up and just stared. The man was sexy, and there was no hiding it. Every time he grabbed at his hair in frustration, his shirt rode up, revealing abs that looked like they'd been chiseled from stone.

Stop drooling, Diana.

He was restless, she could tell. It was funny how she'd already learned to read so many of his quirks and tells. When he was laughing at her, his eyes crinkled slightly at the corners, and he always looked to the side when he was embarrassed. He got twitchy when he was frustrated but eerily calm and silent when he was angry.

Not that she was afraid of him. Wasn't that interesting? She'd stolen from him, and he wouldn't let her leave, but she still didn't feel any fear. It was a bone-deep certainty that told her Rafe would never hurt her, no matter how annoyed or angry he was. It was more than she'd gotten from her own flesh and blood. Her father had sold her to a Russian thug. A man old enough to be her father.

He was supposed to protect her. So much for family loyalty.

And as for her brothers, while they hadn't exactly been warm and fuzzy growing up, she'd never thought they were bad people. Not the kind of people that she'd read about in Rafe's files anyway: men who hurt and abused women, trading them for profit as if they were mere objects to be bought and sold like commodities in their portfolio. Is that how they thought of her? Obviously, they were still doing business with Boris, so they knew about the marriage arrangement.

Would she be just like one of those other poor women who found themselves in a shipping crate being sold to some sick bastard? *Your cage might be more gilded, but it's still a cage.*

When Rafe took her face between his hands, Di started. Then his thumb brushed over her cheek, and she realized she was crying.

"I'm not sure what to do with you, Di. This is a difficult situation. After what you stole and what you now know, you're not safe out there."

Di snorted. "You're worried about my safety after I stole from *you*?"

But she could tell how sincere he was. Something else was at play here. Oh hell, that was the last thing she needed, to start feeling guilty. But there it was. How could a woman not be a little bit charmed by a guy who consistently put her first? Especially one who insisted on looking at her like she was a cinnamon bun that he wanted to lick.

"I'm worried about *both* of us. That information you took is dangerous and not just to me. To other people who won't hesitate to harm anyone that gets in their way. Did you show it to anyone else?"

Di shook her head frantically. "No, I didn't even have time to do that."

Rafe blew out a breath. "Be honest. Because I can't protect you if I don't know what I'm dealing with."

"You don't need to protect me. That's what I'm telling you. Let me walk out of here, and you'll never see or hear from me again. It's better that way."

He rested his forehead against hers so she couldn't avoid his gaze. It was almost more painful to have to look directly into his eyes. She didn't want to see the disappointment or anger there when she'd gotten used to him looking at her with affection... maybe even something more than that.

No, Di cautioned herself. *It does you no good to start spinning fantasies about staying here with Rafe. The only way out of this is to disappear to somewhere no one will ever find you.*

"If you run from me, I will follow. You have no idea the things that people like that would do to you. The kinds of things men like me are capable of."

"No, I don't. Why don't you tell me?"

Di wasn't sure where she got the courage to ask such a question, but as soon as it was out there, she realized she truly wanted to know. She knew that he'd been a killer. He had files on other killers. He'd worked for some place called ORUS, and he'd once been FBI, but she didn't know much else. There was so much information to sift through.

And once she'd seen the information on her family, she'd been too sick to look further. It was clear she should never have seen that information. Rafe kept referring to his past and saying that he wasn't good for her. But what did that mean exactly?

She felt a sudden and intense need to know exactly what Rafe had survived and what horrible things he had done that he deemed beyond redemption. Was it because she wanted to get to know him better or because she felt guilty for not knowing more about a man that she was halfway in love with?

More than halfway, if she was honest with herself.

"Don't ask me that. At least now you still look at me like I'm a hero. If I told you more, you'd never look at me that way again."

When he released her, Di felt like something was being ripped away from her. But it was probably for the best. Although Rafe seemed to think that he could He-Man his way through this, Di didn't want him to. It would just put him in harm's way for no reason. If she just vanished, her brothers would probably assume that she'd found the Jewel of the Sea and disappeared with it. This was about profit for them. If they believed she'd stolen the jewel back, they'd focus their resources on looking for her and leave Rafe alone.

It was the only way to protect him.

"So what do we do now?" Di asked. She wasn't sure what Rafe was planning.

"*We* don't do anything. *I* am going to call off the dogs who would see you hurt for what you stole. *You* are going to keep your pretty ass in this room where you're safe." Rafe's dark eyes zeroed in on her, and she squirmed under his scrutiny.

"Do you really plan to keep me here against my will? How did you plan to do that? Tie me up?" As soon as she said it, she bit her lip, knowing exactly where he'd take that statement.

As expected, his lips curled up into a dirty smile. "I can definitely tie you up. Would you like that, sweetheart? To be tied to my bed, waiting for me to get home and play with you?"

Her stomach flipped at the thought. She definitely wouldn't mind being tied to Rafe's bed, and he no doubt knew exactly how wet just the thought of it made her. Damn him! The man could play her emotions like a violin, and she couldn't afford to get distracted.

But Rafe's distractions always felt so good.

Suddenly the idea of letting Rafe handle everything didn't sound so bad. Di was exhausted. It hit her in that moment just how tired she was of lying, hiding, and trying to determine who was friend or foe. The whole thing was maddening, and it was so tempting to allow Rafe to take over everything while she stayed safely under his protection.

But she loved him. It was stupid to pretend otherwise, and the last thing she wanted was to put him in harm's way. Although she hadn't been close to her brothers growing up, she knew they had always been as determined as their father. They would never stop searching for her, and they would hurt anyone who got in their way. Rafe could take care of himself, but what about the other people she'd met since coming here? She thought of Lucia and her adorable little girl. Then she thought of Rafe's sweet grandmother and how grateful he seemed to have her in his life. He could protect himself and probably her too, but what about the others? He couldn't be everywhere all the time.

"I would definitely like being tied up by you."

His eyes lit up at her statement, and when she crooked her finger at him, he crossed the room in two seconds flat. Di gave in to his kiss, desperate for one last taste of him. He was so hard against her, and she relished the feeling of her breasts pushing against his chest. She ran her fingers through his hair, trying to commit the silky strands to memory. It would be the kind of memory that kept her warm when she was alone and Rafe was just another part of her past.

And then... she kicked him in the nuts.

Rafe doubled over in pain, falling to the ground at her feet. Di didn't kid herself. The only reason she'd been able to get that shot in was because he trusted her and had let his guard down slightly. Something he'd probably never do around her again.

"I'm sorry. So sorry," she called over her shoulder as she ran out. She didn't let herself look back again.

5

If Rafe hadn't been ready to kill Diana before, kicking him in the nuts was certain to solidify that now. She couldn't believe she'd done it.

She hadn't gone there looking to start trouble. She'd just wanted to warn him. But then he'd caught her.

Diana flushed as she jogged up to her door at the motel, thinking about what just happened.

Him catching her, the icy quality to his voice, the distinct heat. When he'd used his arms to cage her against the wall, part of her was terrified. Maybe that was the rational part of her brain talking. But deep down, Diana knew Rafe would never hurt her. *Yeah, instead, you keep hurting him.*

If she had told him to stop or that she didn't want

that, he would have backed off. But she *had* wanted it. She'd wanted him not to be angry with her. She had wanted him not to treat her like she was fragile. She wanted that intensity that Noah and Lucia had. She'd wanted raw, unfiltered, and desperate.

Rafe DeMarco was the only man who had ever given her that. The forceful way he'd gripped her hips and slid home. *Every damn inch of him.*

And she'd come apart. No foreplay, no tender words, no long lovemaking session, nope. Just a quickie against the wall. That had been angry sex. And goddamn it, she'd liked it. *Jesus.* Her legs were still shaking, her skin was still humming, and her blood still burned in her veins. The way his hand had slid into her hair as he had dragged orgasm after orgasm after orgasm out of her with his words, with his body.

What the hell was wrong with her? It was like she needed something real, something tangible to let her know that these few weeks were not a dream, or nightmare. And Rafe had certainly given her that. Judging by the tender feel of her skin, the cocky bastard had left hickeys on the back of her neck! She'd never had a hickey in her life. But the idea that Rafe had marked her, why the hell was that so hot?

Okay. Enough.

She had to stop thinking about that. Because even if that was the best sex of her entire life, not that she had that much to compare to, he was clearly angry with her. *And he has good reason to be.* Yes, yes, details. But she'd made it worse just now.

She'd run from him, and to boot, she kneed him in the balls. Her favorite toy and she'd attempted to smash it. "You need some serious psychological help," she mumbled to herself as she unlocked the door to her motel room.

"I certainly have to agree with that."

Diana whirled at the sound of the voice coming from the corner. "Hans?"

Her brother stepped out of the shadows. "Tsk tsk, Larissa. You've been a bad, bad girl. Imagine our surprise to find you were no longer with DeMarco."

Diana tried to back out of the room, but Jakob was right behind her. "Where you going, little sister?"

She had no choice but to stumble forward into the room. "What are you two doing here?" But after the things she'd learned about them, she had a sinking feeling she knew exactly what they were doing.

Making sure they didn't lose one of their investments.

Hans slid a glance at Jakob, who merely shook his

head. When Hans spoke, his voice was low, angry. "Did you really think that we wouldn't know what you were up to?"

Diana struggled to keep her expression even. They didn't know that she knew about their shady business interests. They couldn't.

"I don't know what you mean. I've been hanging out with an old friend and sightseeing."

Hans chuckled. "I have to admit, I didn't actually think you'd make any headway. After all, we've been trying to track down the Jewel of the Sea for years with no luck. But you managed to lead us right to it."

Her stomach dropped. "I don't know what you mean."

Hans made a face, like he was disappointed. "You're trying to tell me that after weeks of fucking that FBI agent, you have nothing to show for it?"

Oh God. It was worse than she'd thought. They'd been watching her this whole time. And now they thought she had the diamond.

"Listen, I broke into the safe. There wasn't anything in there. There was no diamond, no nothing. He doesn't have it."

She swallowed hard as she backed farther into the room. Maybe if she could get into the bathroom, she could lock herself in. Because every instinct in her body told her she wasn't making it out of this room unscathed if she didn't hide or run.

"You're a terrible liar." Her brother slid the backs of his fingers along her cheek. "My beautiful sister, Larissa. What are we going to do with you?"

"Hans, I—"

He interrupted her. "You know, you make Jakob sentimental? I suggested two years ago we give you to Boris early. The Russian has always had an unhealthy fascination with you. He would have paid extra to have you early."

Diana recoiled. "I don't know what the hell you're talking about."

Hans shook his head. "Of course you don't. And I'm the fool who listened to Jakob. '*She's our sister, Hans.*' Pathetic."

Diana swung her gaze to Jakob. But he looked just as foreboding as he always did. And this time he was standing directly in her exit path. She flinched away from Hans when he tucked his fingers under her chin to make her meet his gaze.

"Larissa. *Where is the diamond?*"

"I told you, I don't have it. Rafe doesn't have it."

Hans laughed. "*Rafe,* is it? Since you are unwilling

to give us what we want, it looks like Jakob and I will have to pay him a visit. And we're going to make it very, very painful. But in the meantime, you don't mind if I go ahead and search your pockets, do you? Because I don't believe you." The last word came out with spittle as he spat in her face.

A shudder racked her body. She turned herself away from her brother as much as possible. But he didn't seem to care. His hands were all over her, patting her down, sliding into her pockets. When he slid into her back pocket, he pulled out the flash drive.

"What is this?"

Oh shit. "It's not anything." She prayed he believed her and wouldn't look on that drive.

"What is this? Did you steal this from him?"

"It's not anything. Give it back."

Hans glared at her. But when he spoke, he was talking to their brother. "Jakob, you have the laptop?"

"Yes."

"Here." He tossed the flash drive over his shoulder, and Diana watched in terror as Jakob snatched it out of the air, then pulled a small laptop out of the inside of his jacket.

They were going to kill her when they saw what was on it. She had to keep them from looking at it. "I told you, there's nothing there." All she wanted was to go back to her old life. Where she didn't know anything about assassins or her father.

This was the kind of man her father had been. Someone who intimidated and terrified. Someone who killed, who stole. Her brothers were made in his image. The man she'd gone to avenge was just like them.

"There's nothing on it," Jakob said.

Hans stared at her. "Larissa, what was on the drive?"

What the hell? Had Rafe replaced it? How could that drive be empty? She'd seen what was on there for herself. People would kill her just for knowing about that drive. "I told you. Nothing."

"Very cute, little sister. When you got the drive, was there something on it?"

She didn't know what possessed her to say it. Maybe she wanted the satisfaction of knowing that he knew he couldn't have what he wanted. Not from her. "You'll never know."

And then it happened. The moment she knew she was going to die. It was sudden. One second Hans was staring at her with cold fury, the next his eyes had gone dead and flat. His hand shot out and wrapped around her neck, squeezing so damn tight she couldn't breathe. The edges of her vision turned gray, getting darker and darker the tighter he squeezed.

Diana struggled helplessly, tugging at the arm around her throat. Then he slammed her against the wall, and her skull felt like it was cracking. He added his other hand and squeezed.

Dizzy. *So dizzy.*

She tried to do a simple pluck with her hands, but she had no leverage; she couldn't even budge her brother's hands. They were so big and beefy they overlapped each other around her neck. Her self-defense training didn't help much when she couldn't breathe.

Arm straight up, drop the opposite shoulder. God, she was tired. She struggled to remember what she'd learned about breaking a choke hold. *Twist the body. Drop the—*

Bang. The crash of the door splintering and exploding open had everyone jumping. Suddenly Hans was loosening his hand, but it was too late. Her vision clouded.

And then all she saw was black.

————

Rafe made a quick assessment as he barged in. His heat-sensing devices had told him there was a guy on the door, so he'd taken care of him first. A quick blow to the back of the head had him crumpling into a heap just inside the door. When he saw that asshole with his mitts around Diana's neck, he let out the rage he mostly tried to keep concealed.

With nothing more than sheer brute force, he dragged the guy off her, shielding Diana with his body.

This guy was big. Nearly as tall as Rafe was. He definitely had some training, but he wasn't a professional.

This would take different tactics. Good thing Rafe had been trained to kill and to do it with startling efficiency. Granted, most of the subjects didn't know he was coming.

A quick glance at Diana told him she was alive—hurt—but alive. He growled in frustration and turned back to his prey. *I'm going to kill that asshole.*

The brute lunged for him, and Rafe deftly stepped out of the way but not before delivering a right hook to the temple. The guy staggered, but unfortunately he caught hold of part of Rafe's sleeve and pulled it down with him.

Shit, scrapping on the ground was not how Rafe wanted this confrontation to happen. Pound for pound, he was too evenly matched on the ground. Maybe even outmatched.

Jujitsu training had never been his favorite. There was something about sweaty balls in the face that lacked a certain appeal for him. But still, he'd been a quick study. He kneed the guy in the groin. And although the move was somewhat effective, it didn't slow down his attacker as much as he would have liked. The motherfucker put his hands around Rafe's neck and squeezed. Rafe had seconds before it was lights out. He managed a punch, but the guy just groaned and continued applying pressure to his neck.

Rafe turned his head, relieving some of the pressure on the trachea. And then he worked his arm up and over between the guy's arms, taking one sharp inhale before delivering a strike directly under the jawline at a pressure point. That loosened the guy's grip enough for Rafe to bring his knees up and dislodge the asshole, flinging the guy over his head.

Once he was on his feet again, it was all about hand-to-hand combat.

Kicks were his favorite, and Rafe wanted to keep the big asshole from delivering any blows. He might be slow, but if he landed a punch, it wouldn't be pretty.

Behind him, he could hear Diana rolling around, trying to get to her feet.

He delivered a midlevel front kick, then went

straight for the knee. Knees were a close-combat tool. But they were effective.

Rafe pulled the guy in close, then used his arm like a bar under his chin directly on his throat. Grabbing hold of his shirt, Rafe used his other arm to drag the big guy forward. He delivered a knee to the stomach, and the guy doubled over. Then Rafe pulled back and delivered a knee to the skull. And it was lights out.

Quickly he turned to Diana. "Are you okay? If you can, get out of here. My car is—"

"Rafe, behind you," she yelled.

Shit. The other guy was on his feet, moving fast. Way faster than his friend. And joy of joys, he had a knife. Luckily for Rafe, though, this guy was not as well trained as his partner. The knife swung down in a wide arc, giving Rafe enough time to just lean out of the way. The edge of the knife grazed his neck, nicking him, but didn't deliver a fatal blow. He probably wouldn't even need stitches. Leaning forward, he used his body to protect Diana and then swept his right leg out from behind him, catching the guy's foot and sending him down.

Rafe was on him after that, going for his knife arm. He applied enough pressure to make the guy scream.

That's right, bitch, call for your mommy.

It was times like this that Rafe couldn't deny what

he was. He was a killer. He enjoyed this. These were the moments that got his blood pumping. These were the moments that he lived for.

He was well aware that there was something wrong with him, deep down. But he didn't have time to analyze that just now. The other guy was quick and had his other arm up, delivering a blow right over Rafe's ear and making his head ring. But there was no way Rafe was letting go of the hand holding the knife. He wasn't getting cut in this motel room again. Not today.

It was that fine line he had to walk between letting these assholes live, well, at least one of them, and burning this whole place to the ground, which was what he wanted to do. But he needed for one of them to talk. Right now Rafe was going to go with the one who hadn't actively been trying to kill Diana when he walked in. It was open season on the other guy as far as Rafe was concerned.

The guy refused to let go of the knife, and he was sick of that shit. While they both wrestled for control over that arm, Rafe made a fist and delivered a jab to the asshole's trachea. Instinctively the guy beneath him reached for his throat and let go of the knife.

Seizing the opportunity, Rafe grabbed his wrist and rotated that puppy all the way around, the sound of the resulting crunch satisfying him. Even as the room filled with the asshole's pitiful screams, Rafe did what he did best. He pinned the asshole's arms with his knees then grabbed him by the ears and jammed the fucker's head back onto the ground. Hard. Too bad they were on carpet. If it had been cement, then this guy would never be waking up again.

Well, he could fix that.

The problem with letting his monster out to play was sometimes it was a little hard to put the guy back in his box. In seconds, Rafe lost track of who he was, what was happening. All that mattered was these people had tried to kill Diana. This guy had hurt his woman. Enraged all over again at just the thought, he pulled out his gun and flipped the safety off.

The guy groaned at the sight, but there was no way Rafe was letting him die yet. "Oh no you don't, asshole. You're going to answer a few questions first."

Behind him, Diana whimpered. Fuck. She sounded afraid. He forced himself to stand and drag his reluctant prisoner up with him while still keeping the gun on his temple.

"Diana—" The words froze on his tongue when she came into view.

The stockier guy had gotten up while Rafe was

busy and now had Diana locked against him with a gun to her skull.

"It looks like we have a standoff."

Rafe clenched his teeth. "Let her go, or your partner dies."

The other guy grinned. "You let my brother go, or your whore dies. See, I can play this game too."

Rafe's finger caressed the trigger. The sound of that asshole calling Diana a whore made him twitch. But he had to be smart. His whole goal was to protect her. To keep her safe. Even if she didn't want his protection at the moment, she sure as hell needed it.

"You really think I'm going to trust you?"

The guy shrugged. "You don't really have any choice."

"I could end your boy and have a bullet in your skull before his body even hit the ground."

The other guy looked at the one Rafe was holding. Ah so this one was the ringleader.

The guy said, "We need information she has. So I would rather neither of us dies at the moment."

"Could have fooled me. You were choking her out when I walked in."

"Well, she angered me. You know how it is with whores."

Again with the stroking of the trigger, but he knew

if he killed the guy in his arms, Diana would be gone. And that would be on him. He had to get his shit under control. He couldn't let his emotions rule the moment.

The guy holding Diana smiled. "Easy now, killer. Let him go. Gun down. You can't win this fight today. We'll come for you both another day."

"You can come for me all you want. But come near her, and I will put a bullet between your eyes."

"You're welcome to try. But in the meantime, gun down. Or little Miss Blond-tits-and-ass goes."

Motherfucker. Diana's eyes went wide, and she shook her head. "Rafe. Don't."

He wasn't sure which one she was telling him not to do. Not kill the guy? Yeah, he was already with that program. Not to save her? She was crazy if she thought that. Like he could just walk away from her after everything? He fucking loved her. Which was inconvenient at best.

He put the safety back on and lowered the gun, letting the other guy fall to the floor. "You shoot her, and you don't walk out of here. Neither does your brother. You make your choices."

"Not to worry, I'll be back for the both of you." The other guy threw Diana down on the ground with enough force to make her bounce.

Rafe sprinted toward her while the other man dragged his brother out the door. Rafe wanted to go for his gun, to shoot the retreating forms, but Diana was his concern now.

She groaned as she tried to sit up. "How did you find me?"

He held her gently even as he systematically checked her for wounds. She would have severe bruising on her neck tomorrow. "I tagged you with something when you were at my place. While we were... busy."

Her eyes went wide. "Are you fucking serious?"

"You can yell at me for that later. I'm taking you somewhere safe. You need to be checked out better. Right now you can talk a little, but I don't know how long that'll last. The bruising on your neck is ugly."

"I can't come with you. You heard him. They're going to keep searching for me. I have to go. I need to run." Then she frowned as if she remembered something. "Did you erase the flash drive?"

He swallowed and then nodded. "Yes. I have a device that lifted the data off of it while it was still on you."

"How did you know I'd have it on me?"

"I figured you came to either give it back or blackmail me. And since you're on the run, the safest place to hide it would be on you. I took a calculated risk."

Her lips trembled. "How am I going to get out of this?"

He stared down at her and brushed a lock of hair off her face. "With me. I'm going help you get out of whatever this is. But first you and I are due to have a long conversation."

6

I t had been a long time since Diana had felt this kind of pain. She reached up to touch her throat only to have her hand tapped by the doctor examining her.

"You will experience a significant amount of pain and bruising. We're giving you a shot to help with that, and I'll leave you a prescription to take over the next few days while you're healing."

Diana nodded that she understood. Rafe had really known what he was talking about when he predicted that she wouldn't be able to talk soon. Luckily, he'd called for a doctor as soon as he'd gotten her to safety because her throat had swollen so much she'd feared she wouldn't be able to breathe.

"Did you have any questions for me?" The doctor

held out the notepad they'd been using so she could respond to his questions.

She'd already forgotten his name, but he was handsome with kind eyes. Rafe had mentioned something about a helicopter, so she could only imagine that he'd had to fly him in from somewhere. He hadn't looked at all surprised when he arrived to find Rafe with a woman who looked like she'd been beaten. Diana couldn't help wondering what his usual patients looked like. Did he only work on shady underworld characters? Just what kind of doctor was he?

After she shook her head that she didn't have any other questions, the doctor turned away to clean up the syringe he'd used to give her the shot and the gauze he'd used to wipe up the blood.

"How is she doing, Doc?" Rafe appeared in the doorway. He'd changed his shirt since the one he was wearing earlier had blood on it.

Blood from the slice on his neck that he'd gotten saving her life.

She couldn't imagine why he'd go to so much trouble for her. If things had been reversed and someone had stolen from her and kicked her in the balls, she'd have dropped them off at the nearest emergency room and never looked back. But Rafe didn't even seem all that angry with her. Maybe seeing her almost get killed had made him sentimental.

Shame swept through her, and she couldn't even meet his eyes. The whole time he talked to the doctor in soft tones, he kept glancing over at her. Diana could only imagine what he was thinking, that she was nothing but trouble and probably way more work than she was worth.

Rafe had been so open with her, and the downside of that was she couldn't pretend not to know how he felt. Rafe had been in the trenches for a long time. The only thing he really wanted was to live a normal life. A safe life. The kind of life where he didn't have to worry about people trying to kill him and where he could go visit his sister and be an uncle to her baby. Even if he said the right things, she knew the truth.

Rafe didn't want this headache in his life. Diana was nothing more than walking, talking baggage. Hunted by her own family and descended from a monster. What could she possibly offer him other than a mess?

After another few minutes, Rafe clapped the doctor on the back. "Thanks for coming so quickly, Dr. Breckner. I appreciate it."

"Anything for Blake Security. Keep an eye on that

bruising." With a friendly wave for Diana, the doctor left.

She moved over slightly so Rafe could sit next to her on the bed. His fingers touched her cheek gently. When she tried to kiss his cheek, he turned away. Diana blinked back tears. She shouldn't be surprised. Rafe had every reason to be completely over this relationship. But that didn't mean it didn't hurt that he'd gotten over her that fast. He didn't even want to say goodbye?

"Don't cry. I don't like it." Rafe thumbed away the tears on her cheeks. Diana tried to wrench her face out of his hands, but his fingers were threaded too tightly into her hair.

He looked her square in the eye. "I know what you're thinking." Diana rolled her eyes, and he laughed. "Your face is an open book. It's not a rejection. I just don't want to hurt you."

Diana nodded, but it pissed her off that he could read her every thought on her face. There were so many things she could never share with him, mainly for his own safety. It didn't stop her from wishing things were different though. She could only imagine a world where she could tell him everything and he could do the same. It was a level of trust that she'd never even dreamed of having with a man.

He continued. "I'll always want you, Diana. But more than that, I want you to trust me. I know there's so much more that you haven't told me. Who were those guys? What did they want? How did they find you?"

When Diana turned her face away, Rafe blew out a breath. "You're not ready to tell me those things. *Yet.* But I hope that one day you will. I'm going to show you that you can trust me. But first we need to get you in bed."

Diana shook her head violently at the thought of being vulnerable while she slept. There was no way to know where Hans and Jakob were right now. Were they planning another attack? What if they came while they were asleep? All the agitation made her blood pulse, and she instinctively put a hand to her throat.

"Hey, take it easy. No one is going to get to you here. Not on my watch. I've got it covered. Unless you antici-pate them coming back with an army? You would know better than I would." He looked at her pointedly.

Diana shook her head. Hans and Jakob wouldn't dare involve anyone else. They considered this a personal family matter. They had two objectives: to get her back to marry Boris and to get that diamond. They'd be pissed that she'd slipped them, but they wouldn't think she'd warrant an army. After all, she was ultimately disposable. Besides, they'd be too afraid their enemies would try to cut a side deal and get the Jewel of the Sea for themselves.

"Good. With the hurting I put on those two, they aren't mounting any attacks tonight. If they do, this time I won't hesitate to take them out."

Diana shivered at the thought. She should probably feel a little more than apathy at the thought of her brothers being killed, but after the sick things Hans had told her today, she didn't know what to think. He'd wanted to sell her. And not to any Russian oligarch. To Boris. She'd seen the kinds of horrors Boris partook in. The things he did to women.

That any man could do that to any woman was terrible enough, but the fact that Hans wanted to do that to his own flesh and blood? It was a close call, but her brothers were almost as bad as her father. *No. They're worse.* At least her father did it for money. They seemed to get off on the idea.

What kind of monsters had her father raised? And what the hell did that say about her? It wasn't just for his safety that she didn't want Rafe to know the men they'd encountered earlier were her brothers. There was a part of her that hated the idea of him thinking she was anything like the rest of her twisted family. Right now she was just Diana, the girl he'd rescued and wanted to protect. If she had her way, he'd never know her as anything else.

The idea took root, and Diana wondered if it could be that simple. Could this be a new beginning for her? Luckily, she'd been smart enough to start socking her money away in untraceable accounts, something her father had encouraged her to do. But Rafe could help her set up a whole new identity, to disappear for real. This Diana could be her future, if she was brave enough to take a chance.

Rafe lifted her carefully and then set her on her feet in the bathroom. He turned on the shower and then yanked his shirt over his head. Diana pulled her own shirt off carefully, trying not to make contact with her neck. Once they were both nude, she followed Rafe into the shower and stood, docile as a child, while he washed her.

She started awake as he was rinsing her and then again as he was drying her outside the shower. Nothing seemed real, like a haze had fallen over her vision and she was observing the scene from afar. It was so confusing when she, by all rights, didn't deserve this treatment from him. He should have been at least a little annoyed that she'd hurt him and then he'd had to fight two men to save her. But there was no indication that Rafe resented having to come to her rescue.

He made it seem as if being there for her was exactly what he wanted to do. No man had ever taken care of her like this or treated her so gently. It was something she could get used to so easily if she wasn't careful.

She had to let him know. Maybe if she warned him, he'd take the threat seriously. "Rafe." Shit, that hurt. And she was tired... so tired. "Danger. Broth— Van—" But her eyes wouldn't stay open, and her damn throat didn't work.

"Shhh. Don't talk. Whatever it is can wait until you're better."

As Rafe placed her gently beneath the covers and kissed her on the forehead, Diana allowed herself to snuggle in the glow of his love and care. But she knew the truth, just like she had known it all along, deep down. Her brothers would eventually come for her and Rafe. And this time they'd be prepared. She had to do what she could to protect him. And that meant leaving him behind.

———

RAFE CALLED on every bit of his training to maintain a calm, cool façade in front of Diana. She was exhausted and in pain. The last thing she needed right now was to see him rage. So he'd tried to lock it down, to save it for when he needed it. Such as when he tracked down the son of a bitch who'd had his hands around her throat a few hours again.

He took another deep breath and brushed a stray lock of silky hair off her forehead. She'd fallen asleep so fast it was almost as if she'd turned off a light switch. That was the sleep of the trusting. No one he knew slept like that.

It warmed him that she trusted him enough that she could relax in his presence instantly without a second thought. But then he told himself not to take it as too much of a compliment. No doubt she was exhausted from her brush with death.

The bruising around her neck stood out against her pale skin, every mottled discoloration an insult. *That motherfucker has to die*, Rafe thought. Diana was a tiny thing, and even though she had this crazy idea that she was a badass, she was an angel, through and through. He rubbed his chest, right over his breastbone, no longer able to hold back the nightmarish images that had plagued him on the whole drive while he'd been tracking Diana this afternoon. A million scenarios had played in his mind as he'd hoped that she wouldn't get into any trouble before he could reach her.

It was a dirty trick that she'd pulled, kicking him in the family jewels, but he couldn't even be too angry.

It was exactly what he used to tell Lucia to do.

The thought of his sister made him think of the man she was married to, his former protégé. Exactly the kind of man with the resources to help him right now. He'd worked so hard to push down the part of him he was ashamed of. The part of him that didn't even flinch at killing. He never enjoyed it. He wasn't like some of the others in ORUS, but for the most part, he slept just fine when he took a piece off the board.

He went out to the living room, leaving the door to the bedroom cracked slightly so Diana would have some light from the hallway if she woke up frightened. He pulled out his cell phone and called Noah. His brother-in-law answered on the first ring.

"The tracker came in handy. I was almost too late, in fact," he said before Noah even said anything.

After a brief pause, Noah cursed. "Shit. How bad is it?"

"Bad. The guys who had her had some training. Not ORUS level but definitely not your run-of-the-mill thugs."

Noah's sigh over the line reflected how Rafe was feeling. From the moment they'd met when he'd been assigned to mentor the younger man, there had been an immediate kinship. Noah had been his brother long before he'd married Lucia. He knew that he would always have his back and do whatever he could to help Rafe out, even when it meant the possibility of trouble being brought to his doorstep.

"I need Matthias." He didn't need to say anything else.

"You got it. Whatever you need, man."

Rafe sighed. The problem was he didn't actually know what he needed. This was unfamiliar territory for him. He always knew what he was doing, always had a plan. Then a tiny, blond slip of a woman had come into his life and thrown him off-balance.

And he loved it.

"Not sure what I need yet. Matthias already ran her, and I know the ID is fairly fresh. So that's a red flag, but there's something I'm missing. She tried to tell me something earlier, but she passed out before I could get it out of her. I don't feel safe with her here."

"Bring her here," Noah said. No hesitation.

Rafe couldn't even respond for a moment. This was the meaning of family. People who were there for you without question, even when it might be difficult. He knew without a doubt that Noah would fight beside him to the death to protect Diana just because Rafe cared about her.

"I'll do that. Thank you."

"Any time. I'll have Matthias on the watch for you. He'll let you in."

After hanging up with Noah, Rafe packed a bag for himself and another for Diana. He could stay at home, but for how long? The truth was he didn't know exactly how compromised his security was from what Diana had done. And even if it was okay, why tempt fate? And he was pretty sure Ian knew where to find him if he was the threat. It was better if he had backup. When he was a younger man, and a dumber man, he'd have stayed put hoping for a fight. But now that he was older and wiser, he actually had something to live for. Something he wanted to protect.

Rafe took their bags down first and secured them in the back of his SUV. Then he came back for Diana. She was so tired that she barely moved as he dressed her in a lightweight sweater and a pair of leggings.

Diana opened her eyes several times as he carried her down in the elevator and then out the garage entrance. Once he had her belted in, he tucked a small pillow under her chin. She smiled softly and closed her eyes again.

Rafe got in the driver's seat, and as he pulled out, he kept his gaze trained on his surroundings and the rearview mirror, looking for any unfamiliar vehicles that might be following them. It was a short drive, but he took a roundabout route, just in case he was being followed. He glanced over at Diana, happy to see that she was still sleeping soundly.

When she woke, she might not be too happy with him, but for now she was safe and content. He could relax once they were at the penthouse. Nobody was getting in there. *Except you that one time.*

The information that Diana had on him could have only come from two sources: ORUS or the FBI. They were the only ones who would have known about his presence on the Vandergraff job that put him in close proximity to that damn diamond.

Plus with Alan's little visit, hell, that couldn't be a coincidence. Rafe wasn't sure whom he could trust right now. And until he was sure, he was only going to trust family. Even if that family included a few trained killers.

So that was where he was heading. To family. To home.

It took them an hour to get there because of the traffic and all the evasive maneuvers he took to make sure they weren't followed. By the time he pulled into the underground garage at Noah's building, Rafe was a nervous wreck. Inching along in traffic had made him feel like a sitting duck, and he'd been looking over his shoulder the whole time, hoping he hadn't missed anything. Now that they were on familiar territory, he finally took a deep breath.

When he parked, he saw Jonas waiting by the elevators. Jonas might not be happy about it, ever since almost-murder-gate last year. They'd had a rocky beginning. But he knew all Noah's guys were loyal. Even if the help was begrudging, he would take any help he could get at this point. *They're your guys now too.*

"Heard you were coming to stay for a while. And that we have a new client." Jonas's hard gaze softened when he took in Diana asleep in the front seat. "Need any help getting her in?"

Rafe nodded toward the back of the SUV. "I've got her. But I could use some help with our bags."

"Of course. You take the pretty lady and leave me with the menial labor. Bastard."

But it was said without malice, and Rafe had to acknowledge that it was an improvement over how he was usually greeted by Jonas.

He truly was home.

7

When Diana finally woke up an hour later, Rafe was watching. He got to see it all, the soft trusting look in her eye as she surfaced from sleep.

Then the exact moment when she remembered everything that had happened, and fear reentered her beautiful brown eyes.

Rafe had no idea what to say to her. He needed her to trust him. And the way they were going, one of them was going to die either trying to run or trying to save the other one. He reached out his thumb and swept a tear off her cheek.

"There are some things that we need to talk about. Things I need to tell you." He sat next to her on the bed, taking her hand. "I don't even know where to start."

Diana shifted so she was on her side facing him. "Start at the beginning." She hesitated. "I want to understand you, Rafe."

The soft whisper hit him right in the chest. Maybe it was an impossibility, but having her understand him was what Rafe wanted most in the world. To have her look at him the way Lucia looked at Noah. To have someone see him, all of him, and still look at him like a hero despite the things he'd done.

"I was a wild kid. Really wild. My parents had just died, and I left my home and everything I knew. I was thrust into a neighborhood that, let's just say, wasn't great. My grandmother was awesome. But all of a sudden, I had to be a man when I knew nothing about being a man, and in reality, I was just a kid. I fell in with the wrong crowd."

She reached over and squeezed his hand. The gentle pressure gave him the courage to continue.

"There was one particularly bad time. I thought I was this big man. Like all the things that I brought with me from Connecticut mattered in that neighborhood. One thing that did work out was this deep sense of justice I had. I was like a teenage vigilante or something."

"That sounds like a TV show."

He shrugged. "Hell, it might make a great TV show

one day. Problem was I was also a hustler. I sold a little weed on the side, but before I knew it, I was running pills and then hard stuff. The kind of people that I associated with, they were the worst of the worst. I saw a friend of mine killed in front of me." He scrubbed his hand over his face like he could wipe the memory away. "That was the wake-up call I needed. I knew if I kept going the way that I was, I was going to die."

Diana put her hand over her mouth. "That must have been awful. I'm so sorry, Rafe."

"I was sorry too. I hate thinking about what I would've put my grandmother through if I'd been arrested, or worse. But after that, I straightened up my act. Focused on school. Went straight to school and straight home. Then I enrolled at Fordham. You know, I thought I was going to have the normal life. Go to school, get some kind of job that paid decently. I worked part-time. It wasn't much, but it seemed to be enough. And then I was approached by the FBI."

Diana froze. He swallowed hard. This was going to be the hard part. Telling her that he'd lied to her. It was going to get much, much worse when he had to tell her about ORUS.

"The FBI recruited young for those that show exemplary skills and aptitude in certain fields. I was a good student. Always had been. That was why Nonna never seemed to know about my extracurricular activities. Because no matter what else was going on, my grades stayed up. I was also a good athlete. Good reflexes. I went through a special training program at Quantico primarily for undercover work. They wanted me to go undercover in a government organization, one that had once worked for the US government but the FBI suspected were taking their own contracts."

She shook her head. "I don't understand."

"Trust me, I'm getting there. The best part about the undercover gig was money. Lots of it. I would keep my FBI salary in addition to the salary that the organization paid me. It was enough to take care of Nonna and Lucia. That was all that mattered to me at the time. And let's face it, I was young. So to me, the idea of undercover work seemed fascinating, exciting. A far cry from the ordinary life I'd been living. I could run into danger but sanctioned danger." He shook his head. "I had no clue what I was getting myself into."

"So you're FBI?"

"I was. I'm sorry I lied to you. It's a long story. I was undercover for a long time. Hell, I'm technically not even supposed to be alive. It's only been a year since I've come back out into the world under my real name."

She stared at him, but she didn't remove her hand

from his. Instead, she watched him intently. As if waiting for him to tell her more.

"After Quantico, I was sent back to school as if that semester had never happened. As if all that training had never occurred. The extra FBI courses I needed to graduate from Quantico, I took through correspondence on weekends. There are a few of us that were like that. All because they wanted us young, fresh. It was strange being back in my normal life. In essence, all I had to do was wait to be approached by ORUS. And just like my handlers said, it didn't take very long."

"And ORUS is that organization you were talking about?"

He lifted his head so he could meet her gaze directly. He needed to be looking her in the eye when he said this.

"It's an organization of assassins. They're a black-ops group working with the US government designed to take out the worst of the worst. The kind of people that you can't even contain in prison. The kind of people doing damage across the world to thousands if not millions."

Very quietly she asked, "So you're an assassin?"

"Not anymore. After I was recruited into ORUS, I started out low level but quickly worked my way up. Most of the hits I was on were sanctioned by the government. I only had problems twice. Once, there was this girl who wasn't supposed to be in the house. When I took out my target, I found her there."

She swallowed hard. "Rafe, what did you do?"

"I knew what the FBI protocol was: call it in, have her taken from her home. Away from any family who might be able to look after her. Have her questioned. After losing her father, I didn't think that was the best course of action for her. And then, of course, my ORUS orders would've been to take her out." He shuddered. "I was a killer, but I wasn't going to hurt that little girl. She was an innocent. It was her father who was the dregs of society. So I put her in a closet and made a point to put the fear of God into her. It was the only way to keep her safe. If she ever mentioned she'd seen me there, both my organizations would've taken action. And I didn't want anything to happen to her."

Next to him, she shook. "You did that to save her?"

He nodded. "I may be going to hell for the things I've done, but I'm not taking anyone else with me. I'm not a complete monster."

Diana closed her eyes, looking pained. "I'm sure she didn't understand at the time, but if she had known, she would've loved you for what you did."

"I'm not so sure about that."

"What about the other case?"

"That's the one that got me killed."

She frowned. "I don't understand."

"It wasn't a sanctioned hit. The leader of ORUS was going after someone who was actually an undercover FBI agent. I tried to deter him, but it didn't work. He sent Noah to do the job."

"Noah? Your brother-in-law? But he runs a security firm."

Rafe smiled ruefully. "He didn't always run a security firm. He was ORUS once. I was his mentor in the organization. I taught him everything. He was like a brother to me. But that day, they sent him to do a job they didn't intend for him to come back from. They intended him to die there. But I was able to stop him from executing the hit. And instead, I died."

"How?"

"I was wearing a special type of ultrathin Kevlar. So when he shot me, he thought he'd killed me. But I managed to live through it."

"Noah killed you?"

"He didn't mean to. It's a long story. But that day, Rafael DeMarco died. The feds had to clean up after everything went down, so I was given a new name and identity and sent to work overseas. But I had no life. No family. No friends other than people I worked with. It's been only recently that I came back into Noah and

Lucia's lives. We brought the leader of ORUS to justice. The organization is still around but with a new leader and back in the fold of the government."

"My head is spinning. This is so much. Why did you tell me all this?"

"I know you have things that you don't want to tell me. Things that you're scared of telling me. Things you think will make me walk away from you. And I want you to know, that after everything I've done, the lies I've told, the people I've hurt, *killed*, there is nothing that can make me walk away from you. I love you. It's as simple as that."

"I want to tell you. I do. I'm so scared."

"I still have my FBI contacts. I can help you."

She looked stricken, like she might be ill. Her skin went a chalky white. Was she afraid of law enforcement? He needed to do something.

"Okay look. We don't have to do anything right this second. All I need you to do is promise me you're not going to run. Whatever happens, you and I deal with it together. And you tell me in your own time."

"Why are you being so good to me?" She searched his eyes, and he smiled.

"Because I love you. You touch me in a way no one else has. And I'm not going to let you go."

RAFE DECIDED that they were past the talking stage. Diana wouldn't understand how serious he was about her until she had time to witness it. There was no greater proof than the past.

He'd seen the look on her face when she found out he'd been law enforcement. It was a look only seen on the faces of people who have been in trouble. Rafe knew what it was like to be afraid of police and other authority figures. Although he had to admit that it was shocking to think of Diana as the type of person who would be a criminal. She kept telling him that she'd done bad things, but he wasn't sure he could believe it. What kind of bad things could she have done before this? If anything, she had been forced to do things for others. He'd seen it before, criminal groups that used innocents to do their dirty work. But no matter what she'd done or what she'd been forced to do, Rafe didn't care. They were kindred spirits.

Once they'd been together for a while and she had assurance that he wasn't going to ditch her when it was convenient, she'd trust him.

Until then, he'd show her.

Threading his fingers through her hair gently, he kissed her forehead. She sighed when his lips met her skin. Rafe almost did too. He was starved for her touch and wanted to wrap himself around her. But it was more important that he not scare her. He had to show her that he could be gentle and take care of her.

"When I saw him with his hands around your neck, my heart almost stopped beating," he whispered before he kissed her again, on her cheek this time.

Diana angled her head slightly to allow him better access, but he tightened his fingers in her hair. He didn't want her moving too much and hurting her neck.

"Shh. Easy, sweetheart. Just let me hold you. I need to feel that you're okay. Need to feel you here with me."

Rafe knew he was rambling and probably sounded like an idiot, but he didn't even care. Because everything he was saying was true. He'd almost lost her today, and if he had, his heart would have been as good as gone. Now that he knew what it was like to love someone, he couldn't imagine going back to his prior cold, hard existence.

"I'm so sorry," Diana mumbled. "You could have been killed because of me."

Rafe snorted at the idea. "They aren't a threat to me, but they are a threat to you. And I'm going to make sure they never get anywhere near you again." It wasn't bravado that made Rafe so certain. It was simple observation. If those goons were anywhere near his level, they wouldn't have had to recruit a woman to do their dirty work for them.

He didn't even want to think of what they might have on her to force her to take a job like that. Did she owe money? He cursed. He could only hope they hadn't kidnapped one of her kids or her parents.

"Sweetheart, how did those guys force you to work for them? They didn't take your baby hostage or anything, right? Because if they did, I'll go and get him for you. Hell, Noah and his whole team will suit up if necessary."

Diana's eyes shone as she looked up at him. "It's nothing like that. I don't have any children, and my family... my whole family is gone now. I'm all alone." Tears welled in her eyes and spilled over. "I don't have anyone."

Moved beyond words, Rafe cradled her closer. "That's not true. You have me, and I'd die before I ever let anyone hurt you. I'm in love with you, Diana."

Rafe kissed her, allowing his lips to dance gently over hers.

Diana clung to him, her fingers digging into his biceps. "You can't love me." She sobbed. "You don't even know who I am."

He moved closer, kissing her the whole time. "I

know enough. I know how I feel when I'm with you. And I know I've never felt like this before."

Diana moaned softly as he put a hand on her back, right below the hem of her shirt. Rafe slid his fingers over the warm, soft skin bared to his touch. He could never get enough of this. She was perfect for him.

"Don't kick me in the balls this time," he warned teasingly.

She smiled against his lips. "I really am sorry about that. I'm rather fond of those, actually."

He pressed against her and was rewarded with a soft moan. "I can tell. I'm fond of every single part of you. Especially these." He cupped her breasts gently, squeezing them in his palms.

Rafe growled as her hands tightened on his shoulders. He loved the way she felt in his arms, her fingers trailing over his back. His eyes closed at the sensation. He could never get enough of her touch.

She lay back on the bed, and Rafe crawled over her. Then before they could get too carried away, he got up and locked the bedroom door. If Matthias or Jonas walked this way and got a glimpse of her naked, he'd be forced to hunt them down. That was the last thing he needed, especially when he was so on edge. They were just starting to forgive him for the misunderstanding when he'd tried to kill them before.

Diana pulled her sweater off, revealing her bare breasts. The leggings he'd put on her before they left were quickly pushed down and kicked to the side. Rafe didn't waste any time getting out of his clothes either. There was a part of him that was desperate for her, that wanted to bind her to him before she figured out what a bad bet he was. No matter what she'd fallen into recently, Diana was a sweet girl at heart. Her innocence shone out of her like a beacon, tempting the darkest parts of Rafe to ravage and consume. He wanted to eat her up.

So he would. Why deny himself?

He settled between her legs, and her thighs fell open to welcome him. When he licked her little clit poking eagerly out of her folds, Diana sighed and squirmed beneath him. Her fingers tangled in his hair as he licked and sucked her to her first screaming orgasm. She'd barely had time to catch her breath before he was working to get her to number two.

"Oh my God, Rafe. That was too fast." Diana panted.

"No such thing as too fast when I want you this much, sweetheart. Plus it just means I get to do it again."

She laughed heartily when his head dipped and he went back to work. By the time she was squirming beneath him again, he was hard as a rock and leaking all over the bedsheets. He rolled on a condom and sank down on top of her, savoring the feel of warm skin against warm skin. When he came down on top of her fully, her breasts were presented to him like ripe fruit. He took a nipple between his lips and tugged lightly. She rewarded him with a throaty moan.

At the same time, he slid into her, growling as she instantly clamped down on him.

"Fuck, Diana. You're always so damn tight." The firm clasp of her pussy held him lovingly, her spasming muscles massaging every inch of his cock.

He wanted to go slow, to savor and comfort her, but it was impossible with his blood rushing at a fever pitch. Diana's nails dug into his shoulders as she rocked her hips, riding the rhythm he set. She was always right there with him, game to go as hard as he was. Before long, they were both moaning, their breath mingling as Rafe thrust into her eager, wet warmth.

When Diana turned her head and screamed as she came, Rafe could no longer hold back. He was surrounded by her and could feel the sensations they generated together all over his body. He was falling into her, and he never wanted to come back.

"Yes, Rafe. I want to see you come too. I want to

make you feel good." Her soft whisper was the last straw.

Rafe roared in satisfaction as the knot of tension at the base of his spine snapped. He thrust once, twice, and then held himself firmly inside her as he drowned in pleasure.

"I love you, Diana."

Her eyes stayed on his as he continued to circle his hips, drawing out the connection between them. Her eyelids fluttered, and she moaned softly when he finally dropped down next to her, too weak to hold himself up anymore. This was what she did to him, made him feel weak but also safe enough to let his guard down.

"Tell me you love me. I know you do."

Without lifting his head, Rafe waited. He probably should have played it close to the vest and not pushed her for more than she was ready for, but he couldn't handle not knowing if she felt the same way. She was quiet for so long, but he knew she'd heard him because her hands had flexed on his back in shock.

Finally she let out a little sigh. "I do love you, Rafe. It's not a good idea, but I just can't help it."

"Good. I don't want you to."

He kissed her gently before disengaging. He went to the bathroom to take care of the condom. By the time he got back, Diana was wearing her sweater again and facing the other way.

He climbed on the bed behind her and pulled her into his arms. "I know you're worried about how things will play out, but there's nothing you can do about it right now. Sleep. No one can touch you here. All the rest... we'll work it out, okay?"

She stiffened at first, but after a brief pause, she relaxed in his arms. "Okay."

———

DIANA STRETCHED AND ROLLED OVER, her hand connecting with Rafe's arm. The sight of it reminded her of the prior day's events. That, along with the intense soreness in her throat. Suddenly alert, she glanced around the unfamiliar room. They were in the guest room at Rafe's brother-in-law's place, hiding out from her deranged brothers. His place was compromised because he was helping her. She couldn't afford to forget that or how much he'd sacrificed on her behalf.

He loves me.

It was unbelievable and something that she didn't think she'd ever get her mind around. Rafe had been a lot of places and done a lot of things. If the things she'd seen in that file were just a sampling of the kinds of missions he'd done, by all accounts he should be hard and deadened inside. But nothing could be further from the truth. He'd held her so gently and touched her like she was the most precious thing in the world.

She didn't fool herself that he was some kind of monk due to his background either. Just because he'd been all over the world doing those top-secret missions didn't mean he'd lacked female company. A man who looked like Rafe, a man with a body like *that*, would never be starved for female attention. But she doubted that he'd ever let any of those women into his heart.

Instead, he'd saved that for her.

Diana smiled to herself, but her smile faded as she thought of all the things Rafe still didn't know. It was humbling and scary as hell at the same time. Rafe had her on this pedestal where he'd convinced himself that she was perfect. All the amazing feelings he had for her, what would happen to all of that when he discovered she was part of one of the most heinous crime syndicates in the world? The fact that she hadn't known about it until recently wouldn't matter in the end because it would still have the same result. Rafe would lose out on the normalcy he'd craved for so long. He said he was retired from the FBI, but what would happen if his old colleagues found out he was harboring a criminal? If he got in trouble for helping her, it would ruin his chances for having a new life and career outside his former line of work.

It was a choice she didn't want him to have to make.

Moving carefully so as not to wake him, Diana slid to the end of the bed. It was a struggle to get the covers untangled from around her legs so she could stand without bringing the entire sheet with her. Then there was the ache in her throat that had somehow transferred to the rest of her body. *Ow.* Diana slowed her movements, trying not to anger the muscles that already felt like they'd been run over by an eighteen-wheeler. When she was finally untangled, she stood up and turned around. Rafe watched her silently from the bed. *Shit.*

"I was trying not to wake you," she admitted.

He only smiled. "I know. You didn't do too badly. It probably would have worked on anyone else. Well, anyone who hadn't been waiting for you to try sneaking out since four a.m."

Diana shouldn't have been surprised. It was nearly impossible to sneak anything past Rafe. He was too well trained for the usual tactics to be effective. Now that he was on alert, Diana figured her nut jab was the last time she'd take him off guard.

"No more running," Rafe said as he sat up. The sheets slid down slightly as he moved, showing off his ripped chest.

Diana sighed as she took in the full view of a morning-after Rafe. The sight was quickly becoming one of her favorite looks on him. With his hair wild and his dark eyes sleepy and shuttered, he was her every erotic dream personified. He was the embodiment of everything she'd wished for as a young girl when she imagined the kind of man she'd marry when she grew up. Diana smiled.

Okay not exactly.

She definitely hadn't thought she'd marry some black-ops type, but she'd imagined someone intense and protective. Someone who'd do anything for her and considered her love as a gift. Rafe was her dream lover in all the ways that mattered.

Except for the part where she could potentially ruin his career and put him and his family in danger.

She shook her head, emotion clogging her throat. The worst part of all this was Rafe thought he was doing the right thing. He wanted to show her that she could trust him and that he would be there for her no matter what. What he didn't understand was that those traits were exactly why she needed to leave.

He would be there for her. In fact, she had no

doubt that he would endanger everything he held dear on her behalf, and she couldn't allow him to do that. She loved him too much to watch him implode his life for a girl who wasn't even who he thought she was. He wanted her to tell him everything, and she knew if she did, he'd keep her secrets. But doing so would put him in an impossible position, forcing him to lie to everyone and to the authorities. After years of being under the government's thumb, she wouldn't be the reason he lost his chance to break free.

She loved him too much for that too.

"You can't keep me here against my will." Her declaration probably would have been more effective if her voice hadn't wobbled halfway through. But damn if the thought of walking away from Rafe didn't make her want to bawl like a baby.

"Can't I? You must have forgotten who you're talking to." Rafe chuckled and threw the sheet off, revealing that he was completely nude.

Diana gulped. "You don't fight fair."

"No, I don't. That's what I'm trying to tell you, sweetheart. No matter what I have to do, no matter how hard it is, I'm willing to do whatever it takes because I believe in us."

She backed up slowly, Rafe stalking her until they ended up pressed against the bedroom door. Her eyes roamed over the ultra-ripped chest that always made her drool a little. Her breathing sped up as he lifted her and held her against the door. Diana cried out. In this position, she could feel everything, the hard bulge pressing against her core and the sheer strength it took for him to hold her up like that.

Can you say, *sexy as hell*?

"Don't go, Diana. Let me fight for you."

"There's nothing you can do," she whispered, wishing with all her heart that it wasn't true. But nothing short of a time machine that could go back and undue all the damage her father and brothers had done would change anything.

"If you're in trouble, my contacts in the FBI can keep you safe. Whatever is going on, you're not alone with it anymore. We can figure it out together. I've trusted you, more than I probably should have"—he looked down at his crotch with a raised eyebrow —"and now I'm asking you to trust me."

For a long moment Diana stared into his eyes. She wasn't even sure exactly what she was looking for, but suddenly she knew this was the moment to stop running. To trust that someone else would actually stick when times were tough.

She ran her hands through his thick hair. "Okay. I'll trust you."

Rafe nuzzled her nose gently with his, the uncharacteristically tender gesture taking her off guard.

"Good. Until then, I guess I'd better deliver on my promise to keep you happy."

Diana's mouth fell open when he nipped her ear. His finger trailed gently over her neck. Then he snatched his hand back like he was afraid he'd hurt her.

"It's okay. You didn't hurt me." She didn't mention that her throat was sore as hell on the inside. It was like having strep throat on maximum power.

"Let's get you some more meds, and then we can return to the regularly scheduled program."

"Oh yeah, what's that?"

"Operation *make Diana come as many times as possible.*"

8

A few weeks later, Rafe brushed his hands over Diana's hair to comfort her. Or maybe to comfort himself. This was so far outside his usual wheelhouse. He'd never brought someone in to the FBI who actually wanted to be there. Although looking at how she was reacting, he wasn't entirely sure she wanted to do this. But she seemed determined to do the right thing.

He could relate. It was a bitch when the right thing seemed like it would tear you apart. But at least this way he could get her protection on all sides. *If you still have any pull.*

"Agent DeMarco. We're ready for you." An agent he'd never seen before hovered at his elbow uncertainly.

Except he wasn't an agent anymore was he? "Okay, we'll be just a minute."

Rafe turned back to Diana. Her dark eyes were red and shiny. She'd been crying off and on since she'd made the decision to do this. He'd called ahead so there was an agent ready to take Diana's statement and open a case for her. She'd be an official informant after this. It was a huge step, but it was likely the only way to get her out of this situation.

He kissed Diana gently on the forehead. "It's all going to be okay. All you have to do is be honest and tell them what you know."

Diana blew out a breath. "I know. It's okay. I can do this."

They stood together, but before they could move, Rafe's phone went off with a text alert. Cursing, he grabbed it from his waistband. When he saw who it was from, he was prepared to blow it off. Then it started ringing.

"Damn it. Hello," he bellowed, not even caring about rudeness at this point.

"Agent DeMarco, it's Emilie Durand. Where are you right now?"

He sighed. "In the FBI field office in New York."

Instead of being annoyed like he'd expected, she let out a huge sigh of relief. "Good. I called because there's been a break in the Vandergraff case. We need you. Conference Room M."

"Give me a few minutes." He turned to Diana.

She must have guessed what was going on because she smiled gently. "Duty calls, huh?"

"Yeah. Unfortunately. If this wasn't really important, you know I wouldn't leave, right?"

She waved him off. "I know. Go. I'll fill you in later. I just need to get this out before I lose my nerve."

The agent who stood behind them was still waiting. Rafe pointed at him and growled, "Take good care of her until I can get back."

The young man nodded frantically. "Yes, sir. Of course, sir."

Diana squeezed his arm. "Easy, tiger." Her whispered words washed over him, calming his agitated nerves. He wasn't sure why, but all of a sudden the idea of leaving Diana on her own made him very nervous. She was clearly capable of doing this. But still, he watched until she went into one of the offices with the nervous young man and then turned to find his way to the conference room.

When he walked in, Emilie turned around. "You aren't going to believe what's happened."

Rafe took a seat at the table, nodding to those he knew around the room, which were quite a few people.

He'd spent enough time in this office lately to have more than a passing familiarity with half the table.

"It must be good if *you're* this excited."

Emilie didn't respond to the dig, another clue that whatever had happened must be big. She leaned over and hit a button on her laptop.

"Good is maybe the wrong word. More like it *will be* good. We got a hit on facial at JFK. We got a hit. Well, two hits."

At that, Rafe squared his shoulders, even as the knot of unease settled between his shoulder blades. She sounded happy. *Too* happy. Like starting an evil empire kind of happy.

"What's got you so happy?"

"We found them." Emilie's smile telegraphed her glee at the find. It was obvious that she was enjoying this.

He held his breath and prepared for her to drop a bomb on him. Some shit like maybe he'd been connected to the diamond after all. But that wasn't what she was saying. He frowned. "Who?"

"Oh c'mon, wake up." She pressed a button. "Look familiar?"

She hit another key on her laptop, and the screen behind her lit up. Then two familiar images appeared. Another keystroke and their names were highlighted. Rafe squinted when he saw the names on the images.

Fuck. Me.

"That's Hans Vandergraff."

Emilie smirked. "And his brother, Jakob Vandergraff."

Rafe could feel the stares of the others, but his mind was too busy racing with this new information to care.

Those were the bastards who had tried to kill Diana.

What was the likelihood that his old case would reappear in his life randomly? He massaged his temple, trying to calm the storm inside. They looked different than when he'd last seen photos of them. Back then they'd been barely more than teenagers. But now they were men. Big, beefy bastards who had learned the tricks of the trade in their father's businesses.

All this shit was coming back to him because of the sins of his past. He'd taken out their father, and now they were coming for revenge?

No, that didn't make sense. Why attack Diana? Despite how strongly he felt about her, she was a recent development in his life. So that made no sense.

Unless this all came down to the fucking diamond.

There were two alternative theories. One, Diana worked for a rival organization, and they had planned to take the diamond from her and were pissed when she didn't have it.

Two, the Vandergraffs were her employers... and well, they were pissed she didn't have it. So what had been their plan? Send in a beautiful woman to distract him? His stomach flipped as he realized why Diana had been so scared to tell him the truth this whole time. No wonder she'd broken into his safe and then run away. She'd seen the evidence that her employers were into way more shady stuff than she'd probably known.

What the hell were they thinking sending someone as green as Diana in to get close to a man like him?

———

Focus, dipshit.

If the Vandergraffs were in New York and had sent Diana, then there needed to be a change of plan. It was likely the FBI might not be able to protect her.

They'll want to use her.

And that was the problem. He understood how shit worked. And with her so close to their clutches, he was afraid for her.

Way to protect her, asshole. You fed her to the leopard instead of the lion. Either way she still gets mauled.

"It's been a long time since I've seen those two. I'm not sure why they're reappearing now, but you have all my old intel on that case. There must have been something we missed. Otherwise, why would they be coming for us now?"

Emilie nodded at someone across the table. The man stood, then made his way to the front of the room.

Alan nodded to Emilie, and she brought up another image. Rafe almost choked when he saw it. The next image was of the Vandergraff girl. The photo was taken at her father's funeral. She looked even skinnier than Rafe remembered her.

"This is Larissa Vandergraff."

Rafe swallowed but kept his face impassive. He'd been well trained. *Never show any emotion.* In the field that shit could get you killed. But internally, he was fucked. If guilt were a monster, it had morphed into something way the hell scarier than even that clown from Stephen King.

"Is that the only picture of her?" His voice was cool and detached, right? He fucking hoped so. "She'd be early twenties now," he murmured.

Emilie smiled. "This is where it gets exciting. The daughter looked like she wasn't included in her father's businesses. She is a typical pampered socialite. Attended all the best private schools. Went to college at the University of Pennsylvania. But after graduation, the girl became a ghost. The brothers must have kept her cloistered; all photos we have of her are grainy at best."

"Is there a point to all this?" Rafe asked.

"Oh yes." She clicked the button on the laptop again. Rafe glanced at the image of Larissa Vandergraff again, and ice settled into his veins. She'd had everything money could buy, but had she had a good life? Was she okay? Had he scarred her forever?

Her dark eyes stared back at him. The same dark eyes that had haunted him since.

Emilie practically danced with barely contained glee. "So obviously this picture is of Larissa Vandergraff at thirteen. You know that." She clicked the key again. "We ran an aging program on this image. Look familiar?"

Oh shit. Hell yeah she looked familiar. *Too familiar.*

Somewhere in the distance he could hear Alan talking even as parts of Rafe's cerebral cortex figuratively exploded.

"The Vandergraffs have done a hell of a job keeping this girl off our radar, but it's likely they might bring her along for a trip to the States. Maybe even as a reward. It's possible that she has no idea what kinds of things her brothers are into. If we can find her, we can use her," Alan finished.

Rafe stared at the large screen. She'd lied to him. *You already knew that.* Is this what she'd been trying to tell him? When he'd told her they'd work it out together? His stomach flipped. She obviously knew who he was. The things he'd done... the things he'd done to her father. How the hell could she stand to be anywhere near him?

Or did she know the truth? If she didn't know the truth about her family before she'd infiltrated his house, she certainly knew now after she'd robbed him and taken the information from that flash drive.

For weeks, he'd been kissing her. For weeks, he'd been making love to her. The woman on the screen was the woman he loved.

When he didn't answer, Alan answered for him. "Since we know the brothers are here, we need to be on hyperalert. But we also need to work every avenue we can to find that woman. She could be the key to cracking the case against her brothers."

Rafe couldn't breathe. Every gasp for air was constricted through the narrowest of passageways. "Can you change the hair color on this thing?" There was a part of him that was still fighting. The part of him that didn't want this to be true. The part of him that knew that it was *all* true.

Emilie nodded. "Yeah. To what?"

"Change the hair color to blond."

Emilie crinkled her brow in confusion but leaned over her computer to execute the command. A few key taps later, the image on the screen was the spitting image of Diana.

Rafe put a hand over his chest, wondering if it was possible to die from shock. All this time and he'd had the key to the case living right under his nose. In his bed. In his heart.

She'd lied to him, betrayed him, and then tried to leave him behind only to come back and ensnare him even deeper. The haunted look in her eyes, it was no wonder it captivated him. It was the same haunted stare that had been with him for ten long years. The eyes that had made him question everything he thought he knew.

The eyes that now made him want to be a better man so he could deserve her love.

"I think I know how to bring the Vandergraffs in."

The room went completely quiet. Emilie sat forward, anticipation on her face.

"You do? How?"

That snapped Rafe out of his delusion. If they were

going to end this, for his sake and especially for Diana's sake, it had to be done right. She was a victim in this whole thing and had been from the very start.

She'd been thrown into hellish circumstances the day she'd been born to a megalomaniac, sadistic monster like her father and then raised with two twisted brothers. But there were others who wouldn't see it that way.

There would be people here in the FBI who saw her as just one more criminal and try to find a way to hold her accountable for the actions of her family.

Rafe wasn't going to let that happen. Diana had been brave enough to come back to him even though she'd been afraid. All she'd cared about was making sure the information she'd taken didn't fall into the wrong hands. She'd tried to leave him because she was worried about his safety. Hell, as little as she was, she'd jumped on a guy's back to fight because she was worried about *him*.

He had to find a way to keep her protected in all this.

"I think I know a way to bring them in," he repeated. "But first I need an immunity deal."

"Why is it you need immunity, DeMarco?"

Rafe's gut twisted as he stared up at the photo. Diana. She was the girl from all those years ago. Some of that pain she carried around was because of him.

There was the part of his brain that had to replay everything that had happened with them since he'd met her. Every conversation, every look, every touch. How much of it had been real?

He shook his head. No. What he felt had to be real. She'd come back for him when she hadn't needed to and the anguish in her face when she'd told him she had secrets, no one could fake that. He knew her by now. This was what she'd been hiding. This was why she was afraid. And she'd come here today to turn herself in for him. To keep him safe.

There was no way he was going to let that happen. At this point, he could give two shits what happened to him. But he sure as shit was going to protect her. But he knew he had to tread lightly. Rafe glared at Emilie. What had he done wrong? Shit, what had he *not* done wrong? The thing was he would gladly go to jail a thousand times over if it meant protecting Diana.

Turning his attention to Emilie, he said, "Nice try. Not for me. In case you forgot, we're on the same side. I've got a vulnerable witness in my protection. And if you come at her this aggressively, she's going to be in the wind."

Interpol chick leaned forward, planting her hands on the center table and giving him a priceless shot of her quite spectacular tits. Too bad the view left him cold. "I'm curious. First how you came up with this magical witness just now? Because in the weeks I've been here, you haven't said a word. I'm also curious about this witness floating on the wind and if you're going to assist her with that." She shrugged. "Because I must tell you, in terms you'll understand, that would be a felony. If you have a witness, you need to turn her over to me. She can blow this Vandergraff investigation wide open."

Rafe bit his lip to hold in a smirk. If only Emilie knew that she'd already seen the witness once, briefly. He doubted she'd make the connection from this old picture to the girl she'd seen ducking down the hall in his condo.

"Are you kidding me? I've been chasing this witness all over town as it is. And if we don't get an immunity deal going, the witness is going to walk and you'll have nothing. So if you want to have access, you'll have to go through me." Shit, he was losing it. But if Emilie Durand thought she was going to waltz down and take Diana from him, she had another think coming. All that woman cared about was cracking her case. She didn't give a shit who she got killed in the process.

Emilie shoved herself back from the table. She scowled while she paced. "You're obstructing an ongoing investigation. Do you know how long I've been chasing them? And you have the ticket and you won't share?"

Alan held up his hands. "Everyone relax. Ms. Durand, calm yourself. Because at the end of the day, your investigation is on the Vandergraffs, not whatever witness Rafe has brought in. If we get the Vandergraffs, we might even get Boris too. That Russian has been on all our watch lists for a long damn time. There are a lot of open investigations we could close. So if I were you, I would listen to what Rafe's witness has to say. Those three alone will make your entire career. You really want to spend it going after one of my agents?"

Rafe breathed a sigh of relief. He hadn't been sure if Alan would back him up. Especially since Rafe had been blowing him off for weeks.

Then Alan turned his attention to him.

"And DeMarco. What the fuck? You have a goddamned witness? You've had one all this time, and you didn't say anything? This is not an undercover assignment. You said you were done with those. You asked me to bring you in from the cold. Was I wrong to bring you in? Was this whole thing a fucking mistake, bringing you back and resurrecting your ass? I know you wanted to see your family again. Tell me I wasn't wrong, Rafe. Tell me I made the right fucking choice, because to keep a witness from me is not a wise move on your part. Were you in the underbelly too long? Have you somehow forgotten that you are supposed to be the good guy?"

Rafe calmed the urge to knock Alan the fuck out. Alan had been a good handler. They'd been through a lot together. But Rafe wouldn't hesitate to clock him if he at all insinuated that he hadn't been a good agent all this time.

Through clenched teeth, he muttered, "Not a mistake. And you'll forgive my lack of trust, considering how Interpol has been turning up at my house hinting that I'm somehow involved in something with the Vandergraffs."

Alan's eyes swung to the left.

Emilie scowled. "I merely stopped by for a drink and possibly some sex. I got turned down on all fronts. *Nobody* turns me down. Unless they're trying to hide something."

Rafe shook his head. "Just not interested. You don't really do it for me. I'm curious though. Was the attempted questioning about the night I killed the old man part of the come-on? Because if it was, you're rusty."

And just like that, her mask slipped. She wanted to appear aloof, but instead she just looked jilted and vindictive. She'd completely forgotten about their audience.

"Shut the fuck up. I know you had another reason for going there. How do I know your little band of assassins didn't turn on you? I know your type, and sooner or later, Alan will know it too. I'm waiting for you to trip up. Once a thief and a murderer, always a thief and a murderer."

Rafe ignored the twinge of pain somewhere near

his heart. She was right. He was a murderer. Not a thief though.

"I'm sorry, but you have to amend your statement." He shrugged. "The term is assassin. An assassin that you and your agency personally used to carry out things that you were too chickenshit to handle yourselves. Any blood that's on my hands is on yours too."

Emilie turned her attention to Alan. "He's being insubordinate."

Alan shook his head. "No he's not. He's a special agent. He's doing his job."

"I thought he was retired!" Emilie screeched.

"That paperwork hasn't been put through yet. Too busy." Alan looked like he was fighting a smile as Emilie's face turned bright red. "You seem to be taking this case entirely too personal. Do I need to take this up your food chain?"

She clamped her mouth shut then. Rafe tried very hard not to smirk at that. Unfortunately though, a tiny one might've snuck through. He'd never thought that Alan's refusing to accept his retirement might come in handy, but he sent up a silent prayer of thanks at his old handler's stubbornness.

"Now, about immunity. I'm not taking you to my witness until you have something for me in writing. And given the Vandergraff activity, I'd hurry."

Alan pursed his lips. For a long moment he and Rafe had a standoff. Rafe refusing to budge. And Alan waiting him out. But eventually Alan reached into his pocket, pulled out his phone, and made a call. "I'm going to need an immunity deal in the next thirty minutes."

———

DIANA'S HANDS shook as she stared down at the paper. "What is this?"

Rafe's gaze was hard and unflinching. She could see the love, but more than anything she saw the determination. He nodded at the man, then the woman. "These are agents Granger and Durand. FBI and Interpol. And this is your freedom. Sign it."

She had no idea what was happening. When they had come in this morning, he'd brought her in, told someone that she was a walk-in, and then some guy had led her down to this office. Which, in all honesty, looked more like an interrogation room, all fluorescent lighting and linoleum floors. He'd told her someone would be in to talk to her in no time. But she had been waiting over an hour.

Next thing she knew, Rafe was walking into the room accompanied by a gorgeous redhead that reminded her of Jessica Rabbit, and a middle-aged, stern-looking, thin-lipped man.

He hadn't said a word, just handed her the paper. Her eyes scanned the document. It was an immunity deal. *Oh hell.* They knew. And now her brothers were going to come for Rafe. Because the more she read, the more she saw the deal was just for her. "I don't think I can do this."

Rafe leaned forward, planting his hands on the table. His voice was soft but pleading. "There is no other choice. You sign this, you're protected. You don't"—his eyes shifted to the left—"and they'll throw you to the wolves. So please, for the love of God, sign the fucking document."

A shiver ran through her, and she took the pen that he offered. This was not their deal. This was not what she wanted to do. But the look in his eyes told her everything she needed to know. That agreement was shit right now. Even though she'd come in here to protect him, he was now the one protecting her.

And from the looks of the other two in the room, she was going to need all the help she could get. She took the pen and added her signature before she handed it back to him. The relief flooded his face immediately, and the tension around his mouth eased. Then he mouthed, *thank you.*

He took the document and handed it to the other man. "Immunity." He turned his gaze to the redhead. "Now you can't touch her."

"Rafe, I don't understand what's happening."

"It's okay, Diana. I need you to tell them everything. All of it. Leave nothing out."

She took a deep breath. "I guess this part you know. My father, he died when I was thirteen. You were there obviously." She cast her gaze downward. "After he was killed, I was sent away to boarding school. After I finished secondary school, I went to Penn. I knew nothing about father's businesses or what my brothers actually did. All I knew was that my father left me a trust fund. He'd always been adamant about that. That each of us have money of our own. He made us memorize the numbers backward and forward so we could do it in our sleep, and we could always access our funds. He set up my accounts, along with my brothers'. So I know their numbers as well. Those will come in handy for you later, so maybe you can track their movements or something."

The redhead, Emilie Durand, scoffed. "We'll need your accounts too."

"You can have it. I don't want any of that money now that I know how he acquired it."

Rafe shook his head. "We'll go ahead and leave

your accounts alone for now. Your mother's family was wealthy. I'm pretty sure she left you some money in there as well. So let's deal with your brothers first, and then we'll talk about you. Continue."

Diana swallowed. "I wanted to find out who killed my father." She glanced at Rafe and then back down to her hands. "I learned everything I could about that night, pieced together everything I could. Hired people to learn more. For months I watched you."

Rafe swallowed hard but said nothing.

She had no choice but to continue. "I figured that if I got close to you, I would have a chance to recover the diamond. So I devised a plan. You were supposed to find me along the side of the road, needing help. I assumed you'd take me to a hotel or something. Once we'd met, I planned to run into you in the city later and strike up a friendship. Only that's not what happened. You took me home. My plan had worked far better than I'd ever dreamed." She waited for him to say something. He didn't, but the muscle in his jaw clenched.

The redheaded agent rolled her eyes. "So you figured you'd flirt with him and that he'd just tell you everything?"

Diana glowered at her. "No. I didn't expect him to

tell me anything, actually. My plan was to get close to him and see if I could access his safe."

She could almost feel Rafe's stillness. This was hard. Too hard. But he knew the story already. So she just needed to get it out. Ignoring the other two in the room, she turned toward Rafe.

"You were different than I thought. And at the beginning, the whole plan was information. Find out who killed my father. But the more I got to know you, the harder it was to imagine your killing someone for no good reason. And of course then there was the safe."

He frowned. "Yes, the flash drive you took."

She inhaled deeply. "That wasn't what I was after. I was looking for my mother's diamond. The Jewel of the Sea. Twenty-five carats. Practically priceless. It used to be in my father's study. The night before he died was the last time anyone saw it. And then that night. After..." Her voice trailed. She took another deep breath before continuing. "After I was told to get in the closet, I saw the person who killed him, running across the lawn. I thought maybe that person had taken it. Then I opened your safe, and it wasn't there."

He frowned. "I never took that diamond. And I sure as shit didn't make my egress across the lawn. It was too exposed. I took the tunnels to a checkpoint about half a mile away and drove out."

She shook her head. "I don't know. That's what I remember. It was a long time ago. At any rate, I started to put the pieces together. While I've been watching you, apparently my brothers have been watching me. They want the diamond even though it was willed to me by our mother. Every woman in my family has given it to her daughter on the eve of her wedding night as a sort of dowry. Apparently, my brothers have promised it to Boris. Along with me."

The redhead leaned forward. "Boris Klinkov?"

"Yes. That's him. After I saw the files in Rafe's safe, that's when I started to realize what was going on. I saw the files Rafe had on them. My father, his business, the trafficking, my brother's roles in it all. I knew too much at that point. Once they found out I didn't have the diamond, I knew they'd kill Rafe and me. I figured if I ran, they would come after me and leave him alone."

"Convenient," muttered Emilie.

"It's the truth. There were other files that I stole." She slid her gaze to Rafe. "Those files, I realized, were really dangerous. I knew I shouldn't have them. I knew if anyone ever saw them, people might die. So I brought them back to Rafe. I told him as much as I could while trying to not implicate him or get him killed." She glanced up at the middle-aged man. "I had no idea what my brothers intended. I had no idea how many people they are willing to kill or willing to hurt. But I knew I had to do something. That's why I told Rafe I wanted to come in and tell you what I knew."

The older man stared at Rafe. "You already had her in here?"

Rafe smirked and shrugged. "I asked for immunity. I just neglected to tell you that she was already here."

The redhead stared at him with a mixture of hunger and fury. Diana didn't like her. Matter of fact, Diana was feeling awfully violent toward her. She wanted Rafe, and the other woman was irritated that Rafe didn't want her. *Yeah bitch, he's mine.*

The old man shook his head. "I swear to fucking God, DeMarco."

Rafe glared at him. "She has immunity. She was going to tell her story regardless. Now I just prevented that one"—he pointed at the redhead—"from using her as bait. That's all. And this was the only way that was going to happen. I know how things work here. How you use people. I'm trying to keep her alive because she worked hard to keep me alive."

"We need to discuss this. In the meantime, neither one of you leaves here."

Rafe stared at him. "Are you fucking serious right now? She has immunity. I'm a fucking special agent."

"You're retired," Alan countered.

"Apparently not yet." Rafe smirked. "I'm running an informant as I see fit. You can't keep me here."

Emilie gave him an evil smile. "Watch us." And she sauntered out, leaving Diana with a fuming Rafe.

10

Rafe could still see Emilie out in the hallway. She smirked at him when she saw him looking. Inside, Rafe seethed. Had she always been so self-serving? There had been a point when she'd fought for the greater good, right? Or was she yet another woman he'd misread?

This situation was going from shit show to a sea of endless floating shit. The last thing he wanted was to be back here. He didn't want to get yanked back down into the bureaucracy. He'd already given one life to the FBI. Wasn't that enough?

And now this shit with Interpol. The FBI needed to work with other governments to get things done sometimes, that was just part of the job, but *he* wasn't FBI anymore. Why did no one get that he was fucking retired? He was doing them a fucking favor. His willingness to help didn't involve an overly pushy, hyper-sexual female breathing down his neck.

He'd been on her shit list since he terminated their fling in Germany. Now she was on the warpath and determined to take it out on Diana... Lara... whatever her name was. He didn't fool himself that they hadn't seen through his story that Diana was just a contact. They weren't idiots. Anyone could see the way he looked at Diana.

Rafe took several deep breaths and tried to regulate his spiking heartbeat. Because it wasn't going to take much to have him hulking out. The last thing they needed was for him to end up in handcuffs. That would probably make Emilie happy though.

"This is bullshit," he muttered through clenched teeth.

Diana watched him warily. He tried to get it together for her sake. She'd been brave enough to come into the lion's den and tell her story, and he sure as hell wasn't going to let the assholes at the FBI turn this around on her. She could have easily disappeared and not told them anything. The information she'd disclosed was the biggest break in the Vandergraff case they'd ever had.

Rafe wasn't going to allow her to be punished when she was only trying to help.

He pulled out his phone and sent a message to Alan, asking him to come back in. Maybe if he offered himself up as a sacrificial lamb, they would let Diana go. He could see the little bubbles that indicated that Alan was typing a response.

Granger: You've really started a shit storm this time.

DeMarco: What the hell is going on out there?

Granger: We're running down the info she gave us. But you have to know this isn't going to be a cakewalk.

DeMarco: Meet me outside. We need to talk.

Then he turned to Diana. He sighed when he saw that she'd curled her arms on the metal table to make a pillow for herself. Her eyes were closed, but she didn't look like she was resting at all. She still looked terrified, but there was nothing he could do about that yet.

"Hey, Diana," he whispered.

At the sound of his voice, she shot upward. "Are they letting us go yet?"

"Not yet. But I'm going to take care of things. Just wait here." He brushed her hair back from her face gently and pressed a soft kiss to her forehead.

She nodded wearily and put her head back down on her arms. When she noticed him staring, she gave him a wan smile. She didn't believe his words, but he would prove to her that he would always protect her.

Now he just had to get Alan alone and figure out how to get them out of this mess. Rafe really hoped he hadn't made a mistake bringing her here. Perhaps it would have been better to have her submit her statement remotely after he'd hidden her away somewhere. Noah could have probably found him a place within a few hours that was untraceable.

He opened the door and stepped out into the hall. Alan was right outside talking to Emilie. He couldn't hear what they were saying, but it looked like an argument. No doubt Emilie was trying to come up with a reason they needed to be extradited back to Canada. When they saw him, the conversation stopped immediately. Emilie glared at him before turning and walking away.

"What the hell, Alan? I told you about her because I trusted you to do the right thing. Hell, I could have just walked her out of here and left you guys in the dark."

Alan held his hands to his temples. "Jesus, DeMarco. You're really killing me today. Do you have any idea the kind of pressure I'm under? These fuckers are wanted by about five different countries for human rights violations, so Interpol is all up in my ass to get this case closed. It doesn't look good that one of our agents has been harboring a fugitive."

"*Former* agent. And she's not a fugitive. Her brothers are the ones listed on Interpol's Red Notice. Not her."

Alan glared at him. "That's a technicality, and you know it. She might not be officially wanted, but she came in with actionable intel. No way her hands are clean in this. You really think she had no idea what her brothers were up to? She had to have known something."

Rafe could already see where this was going. Alan had already decided that Diana was guilty. It didn't matter what he said or how much information she gave them. He was never going to be someone they could count on to help them, which meant that Rafe needed to get her out of here. Now.

The tension in the back of his neck spread throughout his body. If he was going to make this happen, he had to remind them of whom they were dealing with. He'd held the line for more than a decade, working the cases that no one else wanted and the ones no one else had the skills to handle. He wasn't above reminding them of all the bodies he'd buried on their behalf.

Alan must have been able to see the change in Rafe's face. "I hope you aren't going to do anything stupid."

"I already did something stupid. I trusted the system." Rafe glanced at the clock on the wall behind Alan's head. If he sent a message to Noah now, he could have a place ready for them by tonight.

"We're just taking some time to verify her story."

"Why do you need to keep us here then? You can verify anytime."

Suddenly Alan wouldn't meet his eyes. "Agent Durand is more concerned about your friend being a flight risk."

"I probably don't need to remind you that she has immunity. She's not going to run. Besides, I'll be with her every moment."

"You can't watch her constantly. Plus it's not so much her running away that we're worried about. We don't want her contacting her brothers and warning them."

Alan narrowed his eyes and thrust his hands in his pockets. They'd never been friends exactly, but Rafe had always respected him. He was an agent who put the job first and did what had to be done.

"Who is this chick to you? You're really sticking your neck out there for a piece of ass."

Rafe had his hand around the other man's throat before the last word even left his mouth. Alan sucked in a strangled breath as Rafe leaned closer.

"Don't worry about what she is to me. Do your fucking job and stop trying to do mine."

"Is there a problem here?"

Rafe released him, and they turned to see the same young agent that he'd left Diana with originally.

The guy eyed Rafe with trepidation before he spoke to Alan. "Agent Granger, sir. I was told to tell you that her story checks out. She can leave if she's under protective custody."

"She is." Rafe interrupted. "She's with me. And if you need us, you know how to contact me." He turned to leave before he could say or do something else that would get them locked up.

If everything he'd worked for was going up in flames, he'd prefer not to light the match until he was at a safe distance.

As they drove back to the penthouse, the anger vibrated through him.

Rafe hadn't been this angry in years. Maybe ever. And he was angry at everybody. Alan, Emilie, Diana. But mostly, he was angry with himself. *He* hadn't put the pieces together. He hadn't seen how much trouble she was in. He hadn't seen the setup. *But if you had seen the setup, would you have done anything differently?*

Yes.

He would've killed her brothers at the hotel. With his bare hands. Anything to make sure she was safe.

The whole drive back to Noah's, he could feel her eyes on him, watching him. She hadn't said a word the whole drive back home. He knew she was scared and tired, but he didn't have much to give her right now. At least not anything that would come without anger. He needed to process the whole fucking day first.

The moment they returned to the penthouse, he tried to put some distance between them in the foyer. "I'll be in the conference room."

Diana reached for him. "Rafe, I know this is a lot. And I just want to say thank you. For everything."

Her fingertips grazed his arm, and he deftly side-stepped. "I said I would protect you and I am. I'll see you later. See if Lucia or JJ are here. Don't leave." He would've thought that went without saying, but given everything that had happened, he didn't exactly trust her to stay put. Granted, she wouldn't be able to leave. Not with Matthias's eagle eye on all the cameras.

"So when can we talk about everything?"

He shook his head. "I don't know. Not now. We'll talk later."

He was an asshole. He knew it. But he needed some time away from her.

As soon as he was in the conference room, he

sagged against the wall, finally letting the fear, anger, worry, and shame wash over him. He'd pushed her to go in today, and Emilie almost had her arrested. He was fucking pissed at Alan for his bullshit. And the shame, that went without saying. He'd been part of the biggest trauma in her lifetime. There was no saying I'm sorry for that.

Luckily no one was around. From the schedule he'd seen earlier that week, Tweedledee and Tweedledum, what he'd taken to calling Ryan and Dylan, were out on bad-husband-babysitting duty. Oskar was off. And Jonas and Noah were busy with the new trainee assessment. He assumed Lucia and JJ were home, but now that he thought about it, there might have been some fashion thing or other on the calendar.

After nanny-gate of last year, Isabella was with Nonna and the nanny. It was going to be a minute until they trusted a stranger again. Matthias... was on watch as always, monitoring the cameras. And the kid couldn't really judge him, could he?

But after a moment of self-indulgence, Rafe got to work. All he wanted was to keep Diana safe and to find the jewel. If her brothers wanted it, maybe he could bargain with them for her life.

When they'd left his place, he'd brought the contents of his safe with them. He went straight for the safe in the conference room, punched in the code, and found what he was looking for. His files. There had to be something he had missed.

That diamond, he'd never seen it. Why were all fingers pointing to him? Emilie had practically called him a thief. Did the bureau really think he had it in him?

Yes.

If he were being honest with himself, he had been under Orion's thumb for a long time. He could've turned. But hadn't he proven himself by now?

The diamond had been missing all this time. Hadn't he already proven his loyalty to the good guys? He forced himself to focus on the time he would just as soon forget. But as much as he went through the files, through past operatives, nothing stood out. Nothing about that mission at all.

Every single thing he'd been told checked out. Except for the fact that Diana, well Larissa in this case, was not supposed to be at home. Had Orion known? Had he hoped Rafe would take care of her? Or maybe he didn't care one way or the other.

Rafe had gone in through the service entrance when one of the service trucks was leaving. He'd disarmed the security cameras and followed the schematics straight to the office. The old man, as usual, had dinner in the dining room and eventually retired to his office for a drink to start his business calls with his interests in the Far East.

Except that night had been different. That night, Rafe had been waiting for him. And unfortunately, so had Diana.

Rafe scrubbed his hand over his face, trying to get the image of her dark eyes staring up at him out of his head. His mind played tricks on him, intertwining his images of her.

Her dark eyes staring at him full of fear, full of terror, then morphing into the woman who challenged him. To the woman who chased him down a dark alley, hoping to help him. *They're the same woman. You need to be able to merge them in your head.*

He loved the woman. He'd spent too much time worrying about the girl. He just needed to get his brain around the fact that the woman he loved had been that girl. How could she be with him? Knowing what he had done to her father?

Unfortunately for Rafe, as much as he wanted seclusion, the files offered no reprieve. He would need to talk to her.

When he left his office, he found her in the living room, curled up on the couch, WWE wrestling on in the background as she tried to read a magazine. She looked so small and vulnerable. But he knew better. She wasn't that same girl.

She was Diana. She was his. And he needed to fucking act like it. "I think I need your help."

She lifted her head and glanced at him. "You're talking to me now?"

He clenched his jaw for a minute. He deserved that. "Sorry. I was just stunned for a moment. I'm getting over it. Just give me time."

She gave him a brusque nod. "What do you need?"

He opened the laptop and sat next to her, her scent immediately wafting over to him, teasing him, making him forget why he'd come over again. *Damn it. Focus.* "Look, I'm going over that night. And these files. There's nothing there about a diamond. Am I missing something?

She frowned. "I don't know. The diamond is big enough to fit in the palm of my hand. I just remember it being pretty. It's been a decade since I've seen it."

"The only details I have on it were that it was passed down from women in your family for generations. It was a family heirloom. There's been some chatter about it. As you said, Boris Klinkov wants it. And he's making it clear to anyone who will listen. I think he's obsessed with it."

Diana muttered a curse. "Yeah... I saw that in your

files. Boris has no legitimate claim to it without me. And for some reason he wants that legitimacy. I guess I thought you took it. I don't remember registering it was gone until sometime after Papa's funeral."

Fuck. He took her hands. "Diana, I'm so sorry." He shook his head. "I never meant for you to see that."

She nodded. "I'm coming to terms with it after all this time. Since I've been here. Since I met you."

"When did you find out? About your father?"

"The night I broke into your safe. I expected to find the diamond. Instead, I found the files on that organization you used to work for. ORUS. I found out what my father was. That you were sent to kill him."

Shit. "Diana. I'm not sorry that I did my job. I am, however, sorry that it cost you someone you loved."

She cast her glance down at her hands. "I loved him. But I'm not even quite certain that he loved me. Maybe in his own way. But he *sold* me. Like I was nothing. To be truthful, I didn't know him at all. Even when he was there, he was barely there. He spoiled me. Doted on me occasionally. But he never spent any time with me. I don't have any memories of those fond times with him playing with me. My mother though, I have lots of memories of her. And I was relieved not to find her in your files."

"As far as we could tell, she was legitimate. Just had

the misfortune of marrying the wrong man."

"I suppose that's a comfort."

"Please think. Is there anything else you remember?"

Her brow furrowed. "The diamond was there in his office the night before. I saw it in his safe as he retrieved his diamond cuff links. I remember how the moonlight made it sparkle. I asked Papa to tell me the story of how he and my mother met again. He was getting ready to go, and he didn't have time for me."

"I remember. The reason we opted for the hit on the night we did, was because the night before, your father had been at the Renfield Ball with your brothers."

"It was at least there that night. I don't remember much from the night..." Her voice trailed.

Fuck. He was a special kind of monster.

Had Orion known all along that Rafe was working for the feds? If so, then why not kill him? Unless the hint of legitimacy was what helped Orion get what he needed. And maybe casting blame on Rafe took care of two birds with one stone. An assassin made for the perfect fall guy.

"He probably sent someone else to grab the diamond the night of the ball and then sent me to do the dirty work."

"I can't believe that kind of man exists."

"He'll never hurt you again."

She licked her lips. "So if you didn't take the diamond, then what are we going to do?"

"We're going to find your birthright, and I'm going to protect you from Interpol and from your brothers. They only way anyone is getting to you is over my dead body."

———

LATER THAT NIGHT, Diana blinked in the dim light, disoriented. She hated waking in the middle of the night. Especially in a new environment. It was always so difficult to go back to sleep.

Rafe had taken a bedroom next to hers at the penthouse. They had a lot to work out, and he said he couldn't do that in her bed.

She clutched the pillow in her arms closer, wishing it were him. It shouldn't be so hard to sleep alone. It was what she was used to after all. But she'd quickly grown accustomed to being sheltered and cherished in his strong arms. Now she felt so isolated sleeping by herself. Maybe he'd finally washed his hands of her.

After everything, she wouldn't blame him.

Then she turned and he was there.

"Rafe?" She sat up, shocked that he was just standing in the darkness, watching her. If it had been anyone else, it would have been totally creepy, but she knew this was his way of protecting her. He'd keep watch without taking any rest for himself. But she didn't want to be just protected by him. She wanted to be loved by him.

"Please don't hate me."

It shocked her how vulnerable she sounded. But it was how she felt. Every moment without him only drove home how shattered she'd be if he left her. Every moment was a painful reminder of how much he was risking because of her past.

Rafe moved quickly, his legs eating up the distance between where he stood next to the window and the bed. He crawled over the covers, landing on his arms, hovering over her.

"I could never hate you." His nose brushed her cheek, and she heard his quick inhale, like he was taking in her scent.

It was so unbearably erotic, the idea that he wanted her scent in his lungs, that she moaned and moved against him. Rafe growled softly under his breath, the raw sound traveling through her system and settling right in her core. Heat spread out from there, radiating out through her limbs and washing over her skin.

Goose bumps rose, and his breath on her skin, his fingers on her arm, and the weight of him pressing her into the mattress were suddenly all she could think of.

"Rafe, please. I need you."

She clawed at him, unable to articulate the sudden, all-encompassing need she felt. It was like a living, breathing thing, this need to be surrounded by him. Maybe a part of her thought if she could merge their souls together she'd have a piece of him that no one could take away.

"I need you too. Diana. My sweet Diana. You have no idea how much."

For someone like Rafe, a man of such few words, it meant everything to hear that he was just as lost in this as she was. Did he feel the same urgency to have, to take, to taste as she did? Diana gave in to the desire to touch and ran her hands over his thick, glossy hair and down the broad shoulders that sheltered her so wonderfully. Rafe smiled softly at the touch, clearly enjoying the tactile sensation of having her hands all over him. He pulled back slightly and then tugged his shirt over his head.

Diana had gone to bed wearing nothing but a T-shirt, so she yanked it over her head and dropped it over the side of the bed. Rafe stood and shed the rest of his clothes. Diana watched as that beautifully cut body emerged, looking like an avenging angel in the darkness. He was so very beautiful and all hers. *For now.*

She held out her arms to him, welcoming him to her in every way. Rafe took her lips in a brutal kiss, pinning her to the bed with his iron grip on her waist. She gasped and moaned into his mouth, her skin heating with every lash of his tongue and every sinuous press of his thick cock between her thighs. He slipped and rubbed through her wetness, using her own lubrications to ease the way as he teased her. Diana turned her head and bit his arm, thrilled with the dark appreciation that lit in his eyes.

"Take what you need from me. I don't trust myself to be gentle when I want you this much." Rafe lay on the bed and gestured for her to climb on top of him.

Just when she was about to climb astride him, Rafe cursed and pointed at his nightstand. "Condoms. They're in the top drawer. The whole penthouse is well stocked."

The reminder made Diana think of her vomiting that prior day. She put a hand to her belly. What would Rafe think if he knew that he might have already tied himself forever to the girl who'd lied to him and brought danger to his family?

"Diana? Are you okay?"

She nodded and retrieved the condoms from the

drawer. When she didn't appear to be moving fast enough, Rafe got up and took the box from her hand.

"We don't have to do anything. I would never want you to feel pressured."

Diana put her fingers over his mouth. "I'm not feeling pressured. I'm just thinking how lucky I am to have you. To be here right now. The FBI was a wake-up call for me. My brothers would have killed me. I guess it's just hitting me now that I'm all alone in the world."

Rafe pulled her close and leaned down until their lips met. "You're not alone, Diana. You'll never be alone."

Suddenly desperate again, she grabbed him and tunneled her hands in his hair. Their kiss quickly turned deep and hot. Rafe shifted her back and rolled a condom down his impressive erection and then rolled her over.

There was no preamble. Instead, with gritted teeth he slid home. The first thrust almost took her over, it felt so good. Rafe must have felt it too because his mouth fell open. Curious, Diana rolled her hips and reveled in his reaction as he cursed viciously and thrust harder. Moaning softly with every swing of his hips, she strained against him, trying to open herself as fully as possible. She wanted him as deep as he could get. She wanted everything he had to give.

"You're mine now, Diana. Do you understand? I protect what's mine."

Diana nodded as the first wave of her orgasm threatened, the pleasure just hovering at the edge, waiting to crash over her. Like always, Rafe sensed that she was right on the edge. His thumb snuck between them to where they were joined and started circling her clit in time with his thrusts. The added stimulation ratcheted up the sensation until Diana felt the first coil of that incredible tension unwind.

"Rafe, oh my God."

His eyes stayed on her the whole time, as if greedy for the sight of her losing control. It made her release even more powerful to have his eyes on her as she came apart. She shuddered beneath him as he continued to bury himself deep until it finally proved too much and Rafe gave in too. His low growl of satisfaction was almost as satisfying as all the rest. Lost in the sweet aftermath of her own orgasm, Diana watched as Rafe closed his eyes and his jaw clenched. All those tight, chiseled muscles flexed as he thrust deep once more, holding himself inside her for a long time.

Finally he let out a long sigh and rested his head between her breasts.

11

Rafe watched her sleep. Yes, it was creepy. But he couldn't help it. He loved her. He needed to keep her safe. And he would do whatever it took. It was pretty much all he'd been doing for the past few days. When he shifted, the bed dipped a little, and Diana instinctively nuzzled in to him. And what do you know? His dick was ready for show time. *Cool it.* Now was not the time.

She needed sleep. And he, well, he had some calls to make. Rafe wanted to do some checking up on the FBI servers about the accounts Diana had given them. And he also wanted to place a call to Matthias. Because while the FBI had their own people on it, there was no one he trusted more to hack the dark web. The kid was good. Better than good. He was legendary. And these days, Matthias was one of the good guys. At least that's what Noah told him. Rafe trusted Noah with his life. So that trust extended to the kid too.

Rafe slid his arm out from under Diana, careful not to wake her. His dick, displeased about the latest development, instinctively twitched toward her. *Down boy. We have work to do.*

He grabbed a pair of sweatpants and headed straight for his office. Closing the door behind him, he sat at his desk and opened his laptop, immediately pulling up the FBI access. For a long moment he held his breath as he waited to see if his access had been blocked. He knew he'd put Alan in a tough spot by protecting Diana, but it was for good reason, and he wouldn't apologize for it.

He was mildly shocked when he was allowed full access with his full security clearance. While he had the access, he'd take advantage of it.

Rafe pulled all the information that they had on the Jewel of the Sea. And all the information he'd provided around the time of Diana's father's death. He jumped through file after file, eventually stopping and giving up. Without help, this could take weeks. Pulling out his cell phone, he made the call. Matthias answered on the first ring.

"What's on fire?" was Matthias's first question.

"Nothing's on fire. More like low embers."

"You know, funny thing, when you're a right sot, fires tend to follow you around."

Rafe frowned. "Not sure what the fuck you just said, but I'm guessing it was the British version of fuck off?"

Matthias whistled. "Right you are."

"Look, I can apologize again, but I think we both know that if I had to do it again, I would. You would have done it too because you and I are one and the same. And normally I'd be happy to indulge this little blood feud. Hell, anytime you want to throw hands or knives, I'm in. But right now I have a woman that needs protection. And I can't let her down."

There was a pause. "What do you need?"

And that was the kid. Direct and straight to the point. He needn't have worried Matthias would be asleep. From what he'd managed to gather from Noah, Matthias, more than any of them, had a difficult time with the transition to civilian life. He still slept like he could be called on a mission anytime, getting no more than three or four hours a night. Rafe understood the reasoning. That feeling of always being on edge. But there was only so long that the kid could do that. Sooner or later he would crash.

"The Jewel of the Sea. Have you been able to find anything else on it?"

"I've been hunting. Mostly, you know the history behind it. It's been in Diana's family for generations. The thing is damn near priceless. Last appraisal was $50 million."

Rafe whistled low. "Jesus, no wonder Klinkov wants it."

"Tell me about it. Your woman, she's the rightful owner. With that diamond alone, her net worth is astonishing. I'm surprised her brothers haven't tried to take her out."

Rafe clenched his jaw. "What the fuck?"

"Shit. That's not what I meant. It was more of a philosophical thing. Diana's great. Obviously I don't want anything to happen to her."

Rafe snorted. The kid was even more antisocial than he was. "Fine. Tell me some stuff I don't know."

"Well, for starters," Matthias warned, "I had a little unauthorized looky-loo around the ORUS files. I pinpointed a direct moment in time and got out hopefully before anyone knew I was there."

Hell. The last thing they needed was one of Ian's guys coming after them. "I thought you were the best?"

"I am. But Ian might've found someone better. That happens. Part of what keeps me the best is realizing I may not be the best hacker around anymore. So I'm not going to go poking where I don't belong. At least not for too long anyway."

"So what did you find?"

"Orion authorized an agent to go to Austria the day before you did. It doesn't say in the logs what he went for. But he had a two-day turnaround and returned after a trip to the embassy. Very likely, he went for a diplomatic pouch."

"So he did send someone else. Okay. So if Orion had the diamond, where would it be now?"

"And that's the real question. Whoever's got it obviously knows its worth. They would've paid Orion only a fraction of it. But they've dug in deep and have it hidden. And they're not telling anyone that they've got it."

"Okay, keep digging. Because Diana isn't going to be safe until we catch those assholes. And there's an account number I need you to check into while you're at it."

"You got it."

After they hung up, Rafe leaned back in his seat. Okay, with Matthias on the diamond, he had to figure out a way to stop Klinkov and the Vandergraffs. Because there was no way he was letting them get anywhere near his woman.

———

DIANA WOKE WITH A START, the contents of her stomach roiling in her belly. Her first instinct had her checking for Rafe, but he wasn't there. Once her eyes adjusted to the darkness, she saw the sliver of light coming from down the hallway. Her stomach pitched again, and she groaned. Frantically Diana kicked the sheets off her legs, but her foot caught at the end.

When she finally managed to get them off, she lumbered toward the bathroom like a drunken water buffalo. Once her feet met the cool tile, she stumbled in, only just managing to kick the door shut and lock it before she embraced the toilet.

She had her hair up from around her face in the nick of time before her stomach had enough and released the contents of last night's dinner.

Oh God. Why was this happening? All the usual thoughts ran through her head. The kind people have when they were sick and suddenly found religion. Oh God, what did I eat? Oh God, did I drink something? Dear God, is it the stomach flu?

After each heave, more and more contents came up until there was nothing left but bile. And even then, her body had zero interest in stopping. For the next several moments, she dry heaved over and over again until finally her body had nothing left to give.

When she laid her head on the cool porcelain tile, she curled herself into a ball, wondering what she did to deserve this. *You know what you've done. You know how this happened.*

No. It couldn't be. Please God. But she knew it was true. It was certainly possible. And then to screw with her head even more, she felt a low flutter in her belly. But it was too early for that, right? It was amazing how the mind could play tricks on you. She clutched her belly desperately wanting it *not* to be true. But there was also part of her that craved this. She wanted a piece of Rafe.

But how? Stupid question really. If she was pregnant, then it had for sure happened that day she came back to Rafe. That day that she had come back to help him, or save him. The day she'd come back because she missed him.

He'd come up behind her, surprised her. They'd both been angry and scared. And they'd both been desperate. He'd hooked his hands into her leggings and ripped them down like they were gossamer. And then he proceeded to fuck her up against a wall.

It was the hottest thing she'd ever done in her life.

The two of them had gone after each other like animals.

He'd said he wanted to mark her that night. And he had. He'd come inside her. Neither of them had been thinking about condoms.

At the time, she thought it wouldn't matter. There was no risk. But given everything she'd been through lately, she might've missed a pill or two. Matter of fact, she knew she'd missed one when she was at Charisse's. But she'd taken them diligently since then. That had to count for something, right?

No, it doesn't.

She finally managed to push herself up and over to the sink. Halfway through rinsing her mouth there was a knock at the door.

"Hey, baby, you okay in there?"

Shit. She took a deep breath to steady her voice. "Yeah. Fine. I'm just going to take a shower."

"Let me join you. I can wash your back."

No. She was not letting him in here. If she did, he would see something was wrong. And then he would be all over her until she told him. And there was that weird flutter again. It was too soon for that. If she *was* pregnant, and she didn't know anything for sure—*yes you do*—Whatever. *If* she was pregnant, she couldn't be feeling the baby yet. And also, she wasn't sure what she was going to do. She knew she didn't want to tell him yet. They needed to work out what they were doing. Things were far too rocky with their relationship. Between everything, her lying to him, his lying to her, her brothers trying to kill her, the FBI... No, they needed to be on solid ground first. Then she would tell him. But for the time being she would keep it to herself.

"No. You'll get distracted. And then you'll try to make me dirty all over again."

"I fail to see the problem," he said with a chuckle. But still, there was a hint of concern in his voice. She could hear it.

And that, *that* was the reason she wasn't telling him yet. He was so caught up in worrying about her it would be too much. She would tell him. But not until they were more steady in the relationship. She glanced at her belly. Too bad they were on a ticking time clock.

"Very funny. And you hog all the hot water. I'll be right out, I promise." She deliberately injected some levity into her voice, hoping that worked.

"Okay, suit yourself. I'll just content myself with making you breakfast then."

He was going to cook? *Oh boy.* "No, that's okay. Besides, I wanted to do something for you after all the things you did for me last night."

His laugh was low and made her skin hum in anticipation. "Oh you liked that, did you? If you let me, I can do more things for you, and then you'll want to make me lunch and dinner."

"Rafe DeMarco, you are a fiend."

"You better believe it." She heard his footsteps moving away from her, and she sagged against the counter. What was she going to do?

All she knew was she didn't want Rafe to be with her because he felt like he had to be. She was making the right call. She knew what it was like to grow up with a father who tolerated her more than loved her.

She was making the right choice. At least she hoped she was.

Diana took a quick shower, then came out to find the room empty. She could only hope that Rafe wasn't really trying to cook, otherwise she'd have to explain to his family why he'd almost burned down their penthouse.

"There you are!" Lucia appeared in the doorway to the room just as she was leaving. "Rafe was threatening to cook, so I took over. I'm making pancakes and wanted to know if you're hungry."

Diana was helpless in the face of Lucia's relentless cheerfulness. It was so surreal standing here with Rafe's sister, knowing that she was possibly carrying the woman's niece or nephew. Would Lucia be so nice to her if she knew all the trouble she'd brought to her brother's doorstep?

"Yeah, I'm not sure I can eat anything heavy right now. Maybe just some tea? My stomach isn't cooperating this morning."

"Of course. I have this great mint tea that'll soothe your stomach. Come on." Lucia wrapped an arm around her shoulders and gave her a gentle squeeze.

"You've all been so welcoming," Diana murmured, still taken aback by the warm reception from people who had no reason to trust her. Given everything she'd heard about Lucia's life, she wouldn't blame her for being distrusting of everyone.

"Well, of course. I've never seen my brother smile so much. I'd just about given up hope on getting him to loosen up. Clearly you're a miracle worker."

Diana blushed. "I don't know about that."

"Well, I do. He's never looked at anyone the way he looks at you. It's given me hope for the first time in years."

They'd reached the kitchen by now, and they paused in the doorway to observe Rafe from across the room. Wearing loose sweatpants and a tight T-shirt, he looked like a snack while talking to Lucia's husband. Noah was a handsome man too, but he might as well have been invisible for all that Diana noticed him. No, for her it was all Rafe. All the time.

Damn, she had it bad.

"Look at him. He's just... I mean, he can have any woman he wants." Diana grimaced at the insecure words as soon as they left her mouth.

But Lucia just grinned. "I know. And he's found the one he wants. The one who loves him. Nothing could make me happier."

12

Everything was slowly falling apart.

It didn't matter what he tried, Rafe couldn't seem to get his footing. Something was up with Diana. She'd been acting strangely for a couple of days now. Quieter than usual. Watching him warily. Had he done something? Every night they went to bed and made love like they were on fire. Like there was a desperate need to be with each other. To hold on to each other. Almost as if they would never get to do it again.

That shit worried him.

"Is there a reason you're staring at her and not talking to her?" Oskar leaned against the kitchen counter, watching him watch Diana in the living room.

The sight of the big blond man watching his woman made Rafe glower. "Mind your business."

Oskar shrugged. "Sort of is my business, man. We all live here. If you're going to make me watch you moon over your girl, I'm going to have something to say."

"Oh, and you're an expert on love?"

The idiot grinned, and Rafe rolled his eyes. He liked it better when Oskar was scowling at him. It was his default look. And also, the smile was blinding as fuck. Like looking directly into the sun or some shit. It was a good thing he didn't do that more often or all the guys might have to fight him for their women... though come to think of it, he wasn't entirely sure Oskar was into women. The guy was always flirting with him.

"I do happen to be kind of a love expert."

"No shit. I've never even seen you with a woman. Are you sure you're batting for my team?"

"What's the matter, Rafe?" Oskar winked at him. "You worried I've got a crush on you? That I see Diana as competition?"

Rafe shrugged. "I'm cool with it. I know I've got a nice ass. Look all you want. I've been told it's a thing of beauty."

Oskar's bark of laughter reverberated off the walls. "Cocky bastard."

Okay yeah, it was better all around if the German never laughed or smiled around Diana. "With an ass like this, who wouldn't be?" Rafe deliberately wiggled his ass back and forth.

Oskar nearly choked on his apple. "If this whole thing doesn't work out, I've got just the strip club for you. I'm sure you'll clean house." The German shook his head and added, "But the thing with your girl, something's eating you. You probably need to talk to her. You two have done the thing where you don't really talk about stuff, but you just bone. And while that's fun, and there are certain relationships where that's all you've got, you love her. And it's clear that, for some insane reason, she's all about you. Despite my dropping all my best charms on her."

"I told you, *stay the fuck away from her.*"

The German smirked. "See, that's how I know you love her. So if you love her, stop standing around with your dick in your hand, lamenting the miniscule size, and go ask her what's wrong. Or you can fuck it out. Either way works. Talking, fucking. That's what Noah does at least." Oskar rolled his eyes.

Rafe glanced back over to Lucia and Diana. Maybe the guy had a point. Diana looked up at that moment, and their gazes locked. He took a step toward her, and she gave him a brilliant smile before heading toward him.

But then something went wrong. She frowned and

put a hand on her stomach. Then her eyes went wild, and he saw it, panic and fear. A moment later, she sagged to the ground.

Fuck him.

Rafe had never been so terrified. Okay, there was that time at the motel. Oh wait. Also, when he'd woken up to find she'd left him. Damn this woman was trying to give him a heart attack. He ran to her, Oskar right on his heels. Matthias beat them all to her side.

Matthias checked for vitals. Rafe tried shoving him away. "Mine. I'll check her."

Matthias merely rolled his eyes and kept on about his business. "Everyone in this house has had a refresher on CPR, because of the baby and all. So fuck off, and we'll make sure she's okay."

Rafe had never see Matthias like this... *protective.* That was new. But still, she was *his* woman. He didn't like anyone touching her. At that point, though, all he could do was order Oskar to call the doctor.

The guy was gone in a flash. In the meantime, Diana started to come out of it. His name was the first thing on her lips. "Rafe—"

"I'm here, baby. Just relax. I think you fainted. We're calling the doctor to come and check you out."

"No. Don't do that. This is all too much fuss. I'm fine."

Matthias shook his head. "She's not fine. Her pulse is low. She probably has low blood pressure right now."

Rafe stared at her. "The doctor's coming. Deal with it. I love you, so I get to make these calls."

Breckner was at the penthouse in less than thirty minutes. By then they'd moved Diana to the medical bay, and Rafe paced anxiously outside the room while the doctor checked her out. Why couldn't they just have any normal time together? Time when he wasn't terrified something was going to happen to her?

Was this what love felt like all the time? It was awful. The constant worry. The constant fear. He didn't like that one bit. *Yeah, you do. Because it's better than leaving her alone in the world.*

That was true. He wouldn't trade off for peace of mind no matter what. He wanted her to be safe. But watching her fall like that, he'd never felt so humbled. He could protect her against armed gunmen, but if she was sick? He was completely helpless.

The door opened and the doctor came out. Rafe was on him like a fly on shit. "Is she okay? What's wrong with her? Can I go in to see her?"

The doctor patted his arm. "Yes, yes. She's fine. She's doing well. She just needs rest, and I'd like to get more nutrients in her. But right now everything is good. Baby's heartbeat is strong."

Rafe stared at him. "Excuse me? What do you mean *baby*?"

The doc paused. "You didn't know? She's pregnant. We won't know exactly how far along until we do an ultrasound."

Rafe stared at him. He ran his hands through his hair. "How the hell did that happen?"

Behind him Oskar chuckled. "Oh man, this is going to take a while. So a long time ago there were some birds and some bees."

"Shut up," Rafe growled.

Oskar held up his hands. "Sorry man, I was trying to give you the basics. If you don't know how babies get here, I can help. But you have to listen closely."

Rafe ignored him and stared at the doctor. "You're sure she's pregnant?"

The doctor nodded. "Yeah. It's early. Like I said, this is nothing that can't be solved with rest and proper nutrition. She should be fine. I did recommend that she start her prenatal vitamins right now though, especially folic acid."

The doctor left, and Rafe stared at the door in complete shock. He knew how this had happened, of course. That day. He'd shoved her up against the wall.

He'd been so angry. But he'd also known in that moment that he loved her and didn't want to let her go...

Noah's voice was low. "Do you need help? You want Lucia to go in with you or something?"

Rafe shook his head. "I got this."

He pushed open the door of the room then shut it quietly behind himself. She lifted her head and gave him a small smile. "See. I told you. I'm fine." She tried to sit up, but he was on her in a flash, pushing her back down gently.

"You are not fine. Doc said you need rest."

She waved her hand. "Oh, come on. I'm totally fine. It's low blood pressure. There's nothing wrong with me."

He stared down at her, and then his knees buckled. Taking her hand in his, he kissed her palm then placed his other hand on her belly.

When his gaze drifted up to hers, her eyes were wide with surprise and fear. "You know?"

He nodded. "I know."

"I was going to tell you. But I just wanted some time first."

He frowned. "What? Why?"

"I don't want you to be with me just because I'm pregnant. I wanted you to be with me because of me.

Because you love *me*. And we've had too much stuff going on. And this baby I just—"

He swallowed hard. "You want the baby?"

She scrambled backward on the bed and nodded emphatically. "Of course I want the baby. I just— I didn't want to tell you until we knew what was happening with us."

He breathed a long sigh of relief. "Okay. Thank God. Here's what's going on with us so that we're perfectly clear. I belong to you. You belong to me. And I will maim or kill anyone who tries to hurt either of you. Understood?"

Her lips twitched into a smile. "Well, when you put it that way."

Rafe changed positions so he could sit on the edge of the bed. When he leaned down and kissed her on the forehead, he made himself a promise. He was going to keep her safe. It didn't matter what it took.

Even if he had to sacrifice his life to make it happen.

———

RAFE LOOKED down at the hand resting on Diana's belly. There wasn't much to see there yet, just a gentle curve under the skin. If he hadn't known what she looked like before, he might have missed it. But there was no denying the change. A change brought about by his baby. He was almost knocked over by the bone-deep wave of possessive love that flowed through him at that moment.

Mine.

He fought to keep his expression neutral when he knew he must look like a feral animal. Diana could never know the true depth of how he felt about her. If she did, she'd run away at the first opportunity. It wasn't something that he could even explain; it was just a feeling. That she was his to protect and care for. It was the greatest honor and purpose of his life. One he'd perform until he had no breath left in his body.

"I know you said you're okay," he started.

Before he could even finish, Diana glared at him. "Don't start with me. It's way too early for you to go all crazy protective on me. I passed out just because I'm exhausted and overwhelmed by everything that's happened. But I'm fine. Physically anyway."

The thought of her being so worried that she passed out riddled Rafe with guilt. The whole reason he'd encouraged her to go to the authorities was to take this worry away from her. Now she had to fear the very people he'd asked her to trust. The irony in that wasn't lost on him. Nor did it escape his notice that it was almost a perfect mirror of their relationship. When they'd met, she'd thought he was the enemy and then discovered that everything she thought she'd known was a lie.

He had to wonder if she'd hit her limit on trust. He wouldn't blame her for being confused after being raised with the Vandergraffs as her only family.

"I'm not going overprotective on you," he lied. "I just want to make sure that you have what you need. You and this little one." He leaned down and kissed her belly gently. She probably couldn't even feel it through the layers of sheets and clothing, but he knew the symbolism wasn't lost on her.

Diana smiled gently, and the warmth of it was like sunlight. "You really are happy about the baby, aren't you?"

"Of course. Did you think I wouldn't be?"

"I wasn't sure. I didn't dare to hope."

He couldn't take anymore. Rafe climbed gently into the bed with her, hovering right on the edge so he wouldn't crowd her. But he had to be close to her.

"This baby will be the best of both of us. How could I not be happy about that?"

Rafe tilted her chin up gently and brushed his lips across hers. With a soft moan, Diana opened to him. The tip of her tongue touching his set off a powerful hunger. He was trying to be gentle, holding her like spun glass until she tugged on his shirt with far more strength than he would have thought possible. Following her urging, Rafe settled directly over her until he was resting right between her thighs. When his full weight connected with her, his cock pressing against her, she moaned into his mouth.

"Jesus, Diana, you're trying to kill me here. I'm trying to be gentle with you, baby. You're supposed to be resting."

Her arms tightened around him when he tried to pull back. Then she lifted one of her legs and wrapped it around his waist, using it as a lever to prevent him from moving.

"Rest isn't what I need right now," she said in a low, throaty purr.

The husky sound of her voice stabbed him right through the heart. Did she know what she did to him when she talked like that? She had this way of moaning words that made it sound like she was on the verge of coming right then and there. It never failed to jack him up.

"I'm going to give you everything you need, baby. Believe that."

There was no denying it at this point. Rafe tucked his hands under her plump bottom and held her still as he ground against her. She rolled and arched, trying to force him in the exact spot where she needed friction. But Rafe wasn't going to allow her to direct things this time. He was in control now, and there were so many ways he wanted to torment her before he allowed either of them to come.

"Do you know what it does to me, knowing that a piece of me is inside you right now?" He growled at just the thought, stunned to realize just how arousing it was to think that they'd made a baby together.

After losing his parents, there had been a part of him that was scared to love anymore. If he hadn't already had Lucia and Nonna in his life, it was possible that he would have been lost to the darkness. But after meeting Diana, he'd felt his heart open for the first time since. Knowing that she carried his child inside her broke it open the rest of the way, just cracked it right down the middle.

Rafe growled as she shuddered beneath him, and he inched his way down her torso, kissing and biting as he went. Every few inches, he pushed her shirt up higher until she eventually sat up slightly and yanked it over her head. The black bra she wore wasn't the sexy kind, but her cleavage spilled over the top, already looking fuller than before.

If that wasn't a turn-on...

Rafe continued downward, tucking his fingers in the edges of her jeans to pull them off along with her panties. He had a destination, and nothing was going to derail him. He needed her thighs clamped around his head and his tongue deep in her pussy while she cried out his name. Nothing else would calm this raging storm inside.

"Rafe? We shouldn't do this here. What if someone comes to check on me?" Diana panted against his shoulder.

"They'll get an eyeful of something they don't want to see because I'm not stopping. I can't stop. Not now."

She framed his face with her hands, and her eyes softened. Somehow she always seemed to understand what he needed. In that moment, what Rafe needed was to not let go. To hold her and feel that she was his and was not going anywhere.

"I love you, Rafe."

He shuddered as the truth of her words stormed through him. "I love you too. So much."

His fingers clenched under her bottom, and when she gasped, he took the opportunity to kiss her again. She melted under him like hot butter, and Rafe growled at the possessive satisfaction he got from the reaction.

She sat up lightly and tugged at his shirt until he

threw it off. Clothes went everywhere as he raced to get naked too. He wasn't sure if she felt the same urgency he did to be with her. But this was what he needed. Skin to skin and nothing between them.

"Oh God, yes." Diana's voice failed her when Rafe's tongue trailed down her neck.

He took one plump nipple in his mouth and sucked hard. His dick was so hard, but he wasn't getting anywhere near her until she'd come at least once.

Her hips bucked as he kissed her stomach, and he put one hand gently on the swell of her stomach to keep her still, marveling at the hard curve of her belly. Diana looked down at him and then cried out when his mouth closed over her core.

Heaven. He fucking loved her taste. He also loved feeling her clench in satisfaction against his face. He lived for this, feeling the evidence of her pleasure. It jacked him up like a drug. Soon her cries got louder until she slapped a hand over her mouth to muffle the sound. He smiled against her, then sucked her clit gently until she broke beneath him.

He wiped his mouth on the sheet and then moved carefully up her body. Her eyes were wild as he kissed her gently and arranged her legs around his waist.

When his thumb brushed her clit, her eyes flew wide open and she moaned again.

"Rafe, you're trying to kill me."

He grinned. "Only with pleasure."

Carefully he eased inside, gritting his teeth at the tight fit. She was so hot and tight that he doubted he'd last long, but he wanted to. There was nothing he wanted more in that moment than to stay clenched inside her, smelling her scent, and watching as she lost herself to pleasure all over again.

But all too soon, he felt the coil of pleasure at the base of his spine. When he finally let go, he held her gaze the whole time, hoping she'd see his heart in his eyes.

———

DIANA RESTED in Rafe's arms, listening to the soft cadence of his breath. After making love several times, they'd collapsed in each other's arms exhausted. He'd finally fallen asleep a little while ago. Sleep didn't come easily to him, and she understood why. For years he'd been the one looking after everyone else.

It gave Diana immense satisfaction that he trusted her enough to let his guard down.

She traced a finger over his face. His reaction to her pregnancy hadn't been what she'd expected. It wasn't that she'd thought he'd be angry. It wasn't as though she'd gotten pregnant on her own, after all. She'd expected him to step up and take responsibility because that was who he was. But his reaction had gone beyond taking responsibility. He'd been... happy. The joy on his face had touched her deeply, and even now she couldn't quite believe it had happened. They were a family, and Rafe was thrilled about it. It felt like a dream.

She chuckled and only quieted when Rafe stirred. So much had changed in her life so quickly. It was enough to give a girl whiplash. But as tempting as it was to pretend she was in the middle of some fairy tale, Diana knew that her time to enjoy this was limited. Who only knew what would come out of their meeting with the FBI? She prayed they would finally realize she didn't have anything to do with her family.

She could only hope that they would be able to find her brothers and prosecute them. After all the horrible things she'd seen in Rafe's files, she wanted that more than anything. Her hand went to her neck. Even though the bruises were no longer visible, Diana knew that she would always feel the phantom weight of Hans's hands around her throat. It was a stark reminder of what was at stake here.

Her brothers were dangerous men. They needed to be stopped. And she had a bad feeling that they were just getting started.

The nausea rose quickly, and Diana sucked in several quick breaths. The air only made it worse, and she tried to back away from Rafe slowly. As it was, she barely made it out of the room before she felt it coming. She clapped a hand over her mouth as she stumbled to the hall bathroom. Tears burned her eyes as she threw up the remains of her dinner. The morning sickness had been a little better lately, and she'd gotten complacent, assuming she was past the worst of it. But apparently, it had just been a temporary reprieve.

Damn it. It was supposed to be *morning* sickness. She wasn't sure how long it went on before she felt cool hands pulling her hair back.

"It's okay, baby. Here." He wiped her face gently with a warm cloth.

Mortified but too exhausted to put up a fight, Diana relaxed into his arms and allowed him to take care of her. Rafe was so gentle, cleaning her face quickly and efficiently before flushing the toilet. He put toothpaste on her brush and then handed it to her. Diana brushed her teeth, grateful to get the sour taste out of her mouth. Once she was finished, she wiped her mouth on the towel Rafe held out. Then he leaned down and scooped her into his arms.

"Wait! Rafe, you don't have to carry me. I can walk." There was no one in the hallway at this time of night, but Diana still looked around worriedly.

"I'm sure you can. But I like carrying you."

She didn't have any rebuttal for that, so she rested her head on his shoulder as he carried her down the hall and into their room. After being so violently sick, it was a relief to allow someone else to care for her. Being taken care of by someone who loved you was a privilege that she hadn't experienced in a long time. Not that she'd ever been neglected.

On the contrary, her father, and then later her brothers, had paid quite a bit of money to make sure that her every whim had been catered to. But it wasn't the same being attended by paid staff. They'd taken care of her because it was their job, whereas, Rafe had come to her just because he wanted to.

Rafe set her gently on the bed and pulled back the covers so she could slide under. Diana moved over so he had room to get in behind her. When he cuddled close to her, molding himself to her from chest to thigh, Diana sigh contentedly.

"Does that happen a lot?" Rafe finally asked.

Diana nodded. "I'm sorry I woke you."

His arm tightened around her midsection. "Don't be sorry. I don't want you dealing with that alone."

Even though it was a little silly that he was worried about her morning sickness, it gave Diana a warm feeling that he was concerned about her welfare.

"I'm fine, Rafe. It's just part of the process. Although I can't deny I'll be happy when this part is over."

"Me too. I hate seeing you so sick. I just want to take care of you."

They rested together for a long time, just breathing in sync before Diana felt Rafe fall asleep again. She knew the minute he was out because his arm around her waist slackened slightly and his breathing became slower and deeper. Even after being so horribly sick, Diana was truly happy. This right here was everything she'd always wanted. Their little family may have been unexpected, but it was the deepest wish of her heart.

Her earlier worries about her brothers came back to her mind. She cuddled deeper into Rafe's embrace, and even in his sleep, he tightened his arms around her protectively. It wouldn't do to get herself all worked up again thinking about what could have happened, but it was impossible to purge it from her mind. She was tired of running and waiting on others to take care of things.

She wanted to take some of the control back.

Hans probably didn't realize just how much information she knew about him and their family operations. Since he'd never gotten his hands on the information in Rafe's safe, he could only guess what they had on him. Maybe that could work to her advantage. If she could draw him out, maybe they could trick him into incriminating himself in some way. The idea of being anywhere near Hans again made her skin crawl, but it might be the only way to ensure that he was put away.

Her hand went to her abdomen. If he and Jakob weren't put away, they would always be a threat to her and her unborn child, their own niece or nephew. She shuddered at the thought. Whatever fears she had would have to take a back seat when it came time to bring them down. This was about so much more than her personal history with them. It was about keeping her child and the man she loved safe. She looked over her shoulder.

Rafe was devoted to her. If she didn't come up with a way to end things with her brothers once and for all, he would put himself at risk to protect her.

But she would have to be careful and strategic. Leaving Rafe wasn't an option. She understood that now. If she left, he would follow. There was no place she could go where he wouldn't track her and nothing strong enough to keep him away. Especially now that she was carrying his baby. Rafe would only endanger himself more, trying to find her.

Which meant that she would have to come up with a plan to draw her brothers out that didn't involve drawing them away from New York.

13

The next day, Rafe wasn't sure how things would proceed. Now that he knew Diana was carrying his child, everything took on a different meaning. Part of him wanted to scoop her up and hide her away somewhere safe, but she'd never go for that. No, his little tigress wouldn't care for being caged.

Hell, she'd probably shoot him if he even tried it. Rafe grinned. Her feral side was a surprising turn-on. He loved that she was gutsy enough to take on anybody even if the man in him wanted to protect her from everything that could possibly harm her.

But from the moment they'd woken up, Diana had been relaxed, if a little shy. After another bout of vomiting that she assured Rafe was normal, he'd brought her some hot tea and crackers in bed.

Everyone else was busy, and they pretty much had the place to themselves. It was odd for Rafe to not be actively working right now. He was used to keeping busy, but Noah hadn't assigned him any new cases lately. Rafe knew he was probably trying to give him some space to figure out things with Diana.

After lunch, Diana was walking back to the hallway that led to their room. Rafe grabbed her hand.

"Let's watch a movie."

She bit her lip. "Is that okay? No one else needs that room?"

"No, everyone is out on cases. It's just us here."

She relaxed slightly at that, obviously not comfortable in the penthouse just yet, something he hoped would change with enough time.

"Okay, that's fine. What do you want to watch?"

Rafe led her to the sofa in the living room, getting her comfortable and covering her legs with the throw blanket on the back of the couch that he was sure had been Lucia's doing. Then he picked up the remote.

"Let's see what we've got here." Noah had pretty much every movie channel available, so he was sure they could find something.

They were just past the opening credits on a popular new horror movie when Matthias appeared in the doorway to the living room.

"Hey, can I have a word?" He looked at Rafe and raised an eyebrow.

Rafe knew then that whatever he was about to say must concern Diana. "It's okay. You can talk in front of her. It'll save me the trouble of relaying it all to her later."

Diana stiffened in his arms. No one had said anything directly, but he could read her feelings clearly. She wasn't sure who to trust or whether the others trusted her. Truthfully, he wasn't sure if Noah or any of the team had reservations about helping Diana, and he didn't fucking care. They would give her the respect she'd earned or else.

Matthias looked between them uncertainly but then shrugged. "I have news about the Jewel of the Sea."

Diana sat up so fast she almost bashed Rafe in the eye with the back of her head. "You found it?"

Matthias shook his head. "Unfortunately, the news isn't that good. I didn't find it, but I was able to confirm that it was sold on the black market a few years ago. There was a corresponding increase in ORUS financials right after the sale."

"So it was Orion who stole it," Rafe said.

"It looks like it. Not that we didn't already know that. It's unlikely that anyone but an ORUS-trained operative would have been able to pull off a heist of that level without leaving a trace. But still, now that I've confirmed the sale, we have a starting place for tracing the stone's movement. The buyer was in Romania. That's something."

"Yes, it's something." Diana put her hands over her mouth. "I thought that I'd resigned myself to it being lost forever. You'd think it wouldn't be such a huge deal since it's been gone so long. But it's the last thing I had of my mother's."

"We'll get it back for you, baby. No one can trace the untraceable like we can." Rafe kissed the top of her head softly. He would figure out what needed to happen to get that stone back. Just because Diana wanted it.

And because he wanted Diana.

"Sorry to break down like that. It just hits me out of the blue sometimes. How much I miss my mom, I mean." Diana wiped the edge of her eyes with her sleeve. "How did you find out all this anyway?" she asked, looking at Matthias in awe.

Rafe growled under his breath. He didn't like the way she was watching the kid, like he was some kind of wizard or something. Hell, he could have found the information on his own. Okay, no, he couldn't have; he'd definitely needed Matthias's skills on this, but it still made him want to flex for her. He didn't like his woman looking at another man that way. All of a sudden, his internal thoughts caught up to him and he grimaced. He sounded like a kid himself, worried another guy would ask his girl to the prom before he got a chance.

"Yes, how did you find out all this," Rafe echoed, hoping they could move this along and Matthias would leave them alone again.

"Ian has access to all of ORUS's financial records now." Matthias stated it as if that alone was enough explanation.

From what Rafe remembered of his old associate, he wasn't the giving type. He'd initially wondered if Noah had made the right decision in installing Ian as the new head of the organization. Now he wondered if that had been the plan all along. Having someone you knew in the position was arguably better than a stranger. Even if Ian wasn't interested in helping them, just by being a known player he was easier for them to manipulate. Which was incredibly useful.

Not for the first time, Rafe was thankful for the day he'd been told he would be mentoring a new kid. Noah had turned out to be the brother he'd always wished for. Now he was Rafe's brother in truth.

"So Ian just gave you the access, huh?" he teased.

Matthias smirked. The kid reminded him a lot of Noah. He had that cocky bravado that could get you out of a lot of shit or into a lot of shit, depending on how the wind blew.

"I think we both know he didn't *give* me anything," Matthias replied.

Rafe chuckled under his breath. Diana looked between them both curiously. He didn't bother explaining. She'd probably already figured out that very little of what they did was legal, but it was in her best interest not to ask too many questions. The less you knew, the less you were held accountable for.

"So what are we going to do now?" Diana asked finally.

Rafe stood, holding her in his arms. She squealed slightly at the sudden movement.

"What are you doing?"

"Taking my lady back to our room so we can rest. While you're sleeping, I'm going to come up with a plan to track the stone. That's what I do best. Finding things that have disappeared."

Diana looked like she wanted to fight it, but her eyelids were already drooping. "Okay, but only because I'm so sleepy. After my nap, I want to help."

"You're already helping," Rafe replied. But when he

looked down again, she was already asleep, her head lolling against his shoulder.

He looked up to see Matthias watching them with a curious look on his face.

"What? You got something to say, kid?"

Matthias shrugged. "Nothing."

"She's mine. Remember that."

If he'd said that to anyone else, they probably would have peed their pants. Rafe knew he could be scary as fuck at times; it was an occupational hazard. But Matthias just smiled.

"She's beautiful, but I'm not after your girl. I don't do... connections. Not anymore." But in spite of his words, Matthias gave the sleeping Diana another wistful look before he left.

Rafe wasn't sure what to make of that, but he would be watching the kid. This life, it took its toll. No one knew that better than he did. Sometimes he'd felt like he was aching inside for someone to see him, to recognize him as another human being instead of the weapon ORUS had fashioned him into. If he hadn't had the memories of Lucia and Nonna to keep him borderline human, he wasn't sure where he'd be. Matthias needed that even if he couldn't acknowledge it. So he'd be watching.

A weapon, even one that was on your side, needed to be maintained properly, or it became a risk.

———

DIANA WOKE SLOWLY, and it was like surfacing from underwater. But unlike most days, she came out of the fog leisurely, somehow knowing that she was perfectly safe. When she opened her eyes, she immediately saw Rafe standing next to the window. He turned, and a smile tugged at his lips. A smile she could feel from all the way across the room.

"Hey," he whispered, and there was a wealth of emotion in that one word.

"How long did I sleep?" she asked, pushing up on her elbows.

Rafe didn't get to answer her because there was a knock at the door a moment before Noah stuck his head in.

"Hey, we got food if you guys are hungry. But if you actually want any, you might want to hurry. Lucia was craving pizza, which meant that any other suggestions for any other type of food was strictly vetoed. When I suggested maybe we get some veggie stuff or smoothies for her, she threatened to kill me with a knife in my sleep. She was very inventive. Her attention to detail when it comes to maiming is uncanny. Granted, she left her favorite appendage untouched in her gory tale."

Rafe laughed. "You mean to tell me you're afraid of my sister? She's tiny."

"Your baby sister is freakishly strong when she wants something. If you think you can take her, I welcome you to try. As a matter of fact, hold that thought and let me get some popcorn."

Noah ran off, and Diana could only laugh. It never failed to amuse her how those guys communicated. They were all so big and gruff and obviously badass, but then they'd do and say the funniest things. It was nice to see a different side to Rafe as well, one he only allowed to emerge around those he trusted most. The human side.

Rafe glanced at her. "What do you say? Pizza?"

"Sounds like a plan."

He held out a hand, and she accepted it gratefully. Despite the long nap, she still felt exhausted and a little unsteady. They walked down the hallway toward the living room, the sound of voices getting louder and louder as they approached. Diana clutched his arm tighter. It was hard to know where she fit in with this bunch. They were all really nice to her, but she figured Lucia had to wish her brother had met someone without so much baggage. After everything he'd been through, now he was getting dragged back into the mud because of her brothers. Lucia probably wished he'd never met her.

As soon as they entered the room, Oskar gave her a quick grin before going back to his conversation with Matthias. Diana felt her nerves dissolve a little bit as JJ appeared and grabbed her arm.

"We need to get you some pizza before Lucia eats it all," JJ declared.

With a chuckle, she let the vivacious blonde lead her away. Self-conscious over how tired and haggard she must look, Diana pushed her hair back, wishing now that she'd taken a little more time on her appearance. JJ was also blond but the type that looked like she belonged in a music video, straddling the back of a Harley. She was all sex and spice, while Diana suddenly felt about as enticing as dry toast.

Diana accepted the plate Lucia handed her and took one piece of pizza, praying the smell wouldn't upset her stomach. She glanced over her shoulder at Rafe. They hadn't discussed when they wanted to announce their news, and she definitely didn't want to have to explain a vomiting fit to his sister right now. Luckily, the smell didn't bother her at all. Her stomach rumbled, and Diana suddenly realized just how hungry she was.

"Ugh, I'm starving! As usual," Lucia declared before snatching three pieces of pizza onto her own plate. "Everyone talks about pregnancy cravings, but I never realized that you're just as hungry when you're nursing. I'm probably never going to fit into my old clothes again."

JJ rolled her eyes. "Says the tiny girl who still wears a size that I couldn't fit one leg into."

"You look amazing and you know it." Lucia smirked at her friend. "I'm sure Jonas lets you know exactly how much he loves your curves."

Diana was struck with longing as she watched the two friends banter back and forth. With no mother or sisters, she'd always been on her own to figure things out growing up. Now that she was pregnant, it would be nice to have someone to talk to. She wished she could confide in Lucia and ask all the questions that were banging around in her head, but this was Rafe's sister. Would she be happy that her brother was going to be a father? Or upset that he'd knocked up some random chick with a psycho family?

She took a tiny bite of her pizza.

"What's wrong? Are you okay?" Lucia put an arm around her. "I've been meaning to check on you. It can't be easy being holed up with no one but Rafe for company. You know you're always welcome to hang with us if you get bored."

JJ rolled her eyes. "Um, I know this is weird since it's your brother, Lu, but no straight woman would be bored with Rafe. I'm sure he's keeping her... busy."

JJ made an obscene gesture, and Diana choked slightly. Lucia burst into giggles.

"JJ, stop. Don't mind her, Diana. We still haven't gotten her completely house trained."

"No, it's fine!" Diana wiped her mouth with a napkin. "Everything is fine. I've just been tired. But Rafe has been taking good care of me."

Ignoring JJ's raised eyebrows, Lucia nodded. "He's good at that. Taking care of people. Even though he seems all gruff and scary, my brother has always been the caretaker type. I mean, he practically raised me, along with Nonna, of course."

"He loves you so much. I can tell how proud he is of you when he talks about you." Diana glanced behind her to where Rafe was standing with the other men. As if he could sense her eyes, he turned. The air between them crackled with electricity, and she blushed and turned around.

Lucia regarded her with a kind smile. "I'm proud of him too. He's had a hard life, but he's never given up.

Now all I can do is pray that he learns to relax and enjoy life before it's too late. But I can see I don't have to worry about that anymore."

"Oh?" Diana asked.

"With the way he looks at you, my brother is clearly thinking about a lot more than work lately. You're the first girl he's ever introduced to us."

Although everything inside her thrilled at the thought, Diana cautioned herself not to get too excited. Rafe was an extremely private man, and his life was a dangerous one. Of course he'd probably never introduced anyone to his family. But that didn't mean he'd been a monk over the years.

Don't think about that.

Her stomach churned slightly at the thought of Rafe with other women. But he wasn't with those women now. He was with her. He loved her. No matter what was going on around them, the two of them together was a good thing. And as much as he was determined to protect her, she felt just as strongly about him. She glanced over at Lucia and JJ, playfully bickering over the last slice of pizza.

All of them. They were his family, and they would be her baby's family. The very thing she'd always wanted was so close she could taste it.

She wouldn't let anything get in the way.

———

"Meet in the office in five."

Rafe looked up at Noah's softly muttered words. He glanced over where the girls were chatting and laughing, the pizza long gone.

He didn't want to leave Diana. It was stupid but he worried about her whenever she was out of his sight. But when Noah called a meeting, it was always about something important. He couldn't take chances with her safety. So he followed his best friend down the hall to his office. Matthias, Ryan, Dylan and Oskar were already there waiting.

Noah sat behind his desk, his face grave. "We need to strategize. The Vandergraffs will make a move eventually. We have to be ready."

It should have given him comfort to see that the others were taking this as seriously as he was. But all that registered was a pervasive sense of *fear*.

It was an unfamiliar feeling, this helplessness. He would do anything to protect her, but for the first time he worried that his best wouldn't be good enough. There were simply too many variables at play between her brothers, the FBI and Interpol up their asses, and any others who might think she knew where the damn diamond was. Threats were everywhere, and he was fighting his instinct to take Diana away somewhere and disappear.

But she deserved better than that. A life on the run was no life at all. He thought back to how she'd looked earlier, laughing with his sister and JJ. This was what she needed. Family. Friends. Security.

Things he could give her if he played his cards right.

"Rafe?"

He glanced up at the sound of his name.

Noah was watching him with knowing eyes. "I know what you're thinking. Running won't fix this." He stood and came from behind the desk.

"What else can I do? She's in danger here, and being with me is likely only going to bring more heat down on her."

"That's not true." Noah clapped a hand on his shoulder, as if he could keep Rafe there through sheer force of will. "You are probably the best thing for her right now. Who the hell else could protect her the way you can?"

Rafe sighed. "That's all I want. To protect her. But how do I do that when we have heat coming from all sides? She's too good to live like this."

Oskar leaned back against the far wall. "Am I the only one who's going to say it?" He looked around, and they all stopped what they were doing to glare at him.

Rafe growled out. "Say what you want to say, Oskar. No one has time for your bullshit tonight."

"I'm glad to see someone here is PMSing. Would you like a Midol?"

Rafe flipped him off. "Fuck you."

"I'm sure you would enjoy it very much."

Normally, Rafe would let him mouth off and let his annoyance slide. But tonight Rafe was too raw. He kept thinking about what could have happened if he hadn't been there when her brothers grabbed her. What if he'd lost her before they'd even had any time together? Before he'd known she carried his child? He was far too raw, too emotional.

Noah put a hand on his chest. "You, chill out." He turned his attention to Oskar. "And what the fuck are you thinking?"

"Her brothers aren't just going to give up."

Rafe was a hair away from shoving Noah's hand off his chest and going after the German to work out some of his angry frustration, but Noah's hand stayed steady. So Rafe had to dial it back a notch.

Rafe growled through clenched teeth. "You got an idea, or you just enjoy stating the obvious?"

Oskar grinned. "I'm so glad you asked about an idea. Because I do happen to have one."

Noah rolled his eyes. "Cut the shit, Oskar. Spill it."

"They want her. So we allow them to get back what they want."

For a long moment Rafe was certain he hadn't heard correctly. Then the words started to filter in, and it took Noah, Matthias and Dylan to stop him from vaulting across the room.

"You want to use her as bait? *That's my fucking girl.* She's pregnant, asshole."

Noah's jaw unhinged. Ryan and Dylan exchanged glances. He couldn't read Matthias's expression, but that was par for the course.

Oskar, ever dry, just said, "Well, congrats. So how long before you teach the kid to kill someone in their sleep?"

Noah growled at Oskar. "Can it, Viking." He shoved Rafe back. "Rafe, we get it. No one is going to use *anyone* as bait." He nailed Oskar with a hard look that clearly stated he'd *better* not be suggesting that.

Matthias was actually surprisingly strong, and he was taking the brunt of holding back Rafe from annihilating the German's face. "If she were your woman, would you be so eager to put her in the line of fire?"

Oskar shrugged. "If it would get the job done, I'd do what I needed to do. I wouldn't make it personal."

"We don't put family in the line of fire," Noah reminded him.

"He's not my damn family," Oskar muttered but not so quietly that Rafe didn't hear him.

"She's my family, dumbass!" Rafe raged.

Noah looked like he was ready to let him go and take Oskar out for that comment.

Oskar held up his hands. "Sorry. I'm just saying, we would all be there protecting her. We'd set a trap. We have to do something. Right now we're sitting ducks."

Rafe shoved everybody off him, grappling for a moment with Matthias before the kid finally let him go and shoved him toward the door.

Noah glared at him. "Go cool off. No one's using anyone as bait. We're going to find another solution." He turned his attention back to Oskar. "You come up with another brilliant idea. One that doesn't involve getting one of the family killed."

Rafe wrenched open the office door. He had to find Diana. He wasn't letting her get hurt. He wasn't letting his child get hurt.

Over his dead body.

14

D iana heard the door slam from the living room. She left Lucia with JJ and went to see what was wrong. She immediately knew something was up when she saw Noah and a few of the other guys watching her from the hallway with blank expressions. She eventually found Rafe in their bedroom, pacing.

She watched him for a long moment before speaking. "You want to talk about what's going on?"

"No."

Diana folded her arms and leaned against the doorframe. "Hey, I'm just trying to help you. Obviously something is going on." She swallowed. "Is it my brothers? Have you found them?"

He turned and met her gaze, shaking his head

slowly. "No, we haven't. I'm just frustrated with the whole thing, that's all."

She nodded as she rocked back and forth on her heels. "I just wish I could help in some way. I wish that none of you were in danger because of me."

Rafe stalked toward her, then wrapped his arms around her, enveloping her in his warmth. "None of this is your fault. You didn't do anything wrong."

She wasn't willing to dismiss what she was feeling that easily. "But this is my family. In so many ways my ignorance makes me complicit. I saw what I wanted. So maybe I need to help stop it. *I need to do something.*"

He searched her face. "Did Oskar say something to you?"

Diana frowned. "Why would Oskar say something to me?"

Rafe shook his head. "Never mind."

"Rafe, we can't keep doing this. This is no way to live, looking over our shoulders and keeping us under lock and key. It's time to go on the offensive, or it's time to put some distance between me and the rest of you. I'm the one they want. The smart choice is to have me leave."

He scowled at her. "There's nothing smart about it. This penthouse is a fortress. You're safest here. Even clients are only ever shown the conference room.

There is no way I'm letting you out of my sight, so you're just going to have to deal with it."

She narrowed her gaze. "Do I have to remind you that I researched you for over a year and none of you were any the wiser? I am a fighter. I know how to take care of myself. You can take your damsel-in-distress-protection shit and shove it. I am your partner. Stop trying to protect me."

His chuckle was harsh. "Things are different now, Diana. You're pregnant. They can hurt you."

She hated that he was right, but she didn't want to concede that point. "They got the jump on me last time. I admit that."

"I know, baby. That's why staying here is for the best. Noah and the others can help me protect you. Leaving doesn't make them any safer. Your brothers already know you're connected to me, so everyone here is still in danger even if you leave."

She buried her face in his chest. "I feel terrible. Even if I'm not directly responsible, I feel like I need to do something."

"You're doing everything you can. We've already talked to the FBI. You've given them all the information you have. It's up to them to take action."

"Yeah, but still. My brothers are after *me*. Maybe you guys could use me."

He grabbed her shoulders. "I am not using you as bait. No more talking to Oskar. He was the one who came up with this stupid bait idea."

"So that's why you look so pissed. Oskar didn't say anything to me but it's not the worst idea in the world. If you won't let me draw them away from everyone, then let me do this. They want me. And they'll take me any way they can get me. If you know they are going to keep coming, it's much better if it's on our terms, don't you think?"

His thumb slid over her bare skin. "You truly have no idea how much you mean to me, do you? I can't lose you."

Diana stepped into his space and wrapped her arms around his waist. "I'm not going anywhere. I'm just saying we need to try to do *something*."

"And we will. We'll brainstorm some ideas. Right now I just need to be close to you. The idea of losing you terrifies me."

"You're not going to lose me. We're going to find a way to end this."

Rafe kissed her. As always, his lips were expert over hers. His hands gently held and caressed her face as they kissed, and the tender action made her melt from the inside out. Diana tugged his head back down and fused her lips with his, raising her hips to meet the hard length of him.

A growl bubbled up from deep in his throat. He tugged at the hem of her tank top, untucking it from her jeans and exposing her belly. The moment his hands met with skin, her breath caught.

Every time he touched her, it sent a zing of pleasure to her core. She wondered if that would ever end. His roving hands traveled up her rib cage. He muttered something that was part epithet, part homage as his thumb came into contact with the bare flesh of her breast.

When he didn't continue, she squirmed under him, and he chuckled. When his thumb traced a circle over her nipple, Diana arched her back in an attempt to get closer. The peak stiffened in response as her core pulsed. When she groaned, he repeated the action.

Desperate to get closer, Diana pressed into him. With a low growl, he picked her up and kicked the door shut behind them. He wasted no time once he deposited her on the bed, going right back to driving her crazy by teasing her nipples.

She gasped out his name. On his third pass, he tugged the nub between his thumb and forefinger, and she moaned his name as her hips rode his thigh.

With a curse, he yanked her tank over her head.

When her heavy breasts spilled free, Rafe's muttered "fuck" made her blush.

"You are so beautiful," he muttered and kissed her belly button. As he traced kisses from her stomach up her rib cage, Diana arched her back as each kiss drifted closer to her breasts. When his hot mouth closed over a nipple, her core contracted and released. Moist heat dampened her panties, and she rolled her hips into his as he suckled one breast, his palm closed over the other.

Diana pulled at his T-shirt and dragged the material over his head, exposing an expanse of bare torso.

Her hands tentatively roamed over the nape of his neck and his back, exploring the muscles of his deltoids. With each stroke she could feel him shiver.

Wrapping his arms around her, Rafe rolled them both over so that she sat on top. God, he was big. Broad shoulders and a wingspan like a swimmer. Thick muscles corded his neck and his broad chest. They rippled with every intake of breath as her fingertips glided over his skin. When her hands shifted down to his abs, he sucked in a breath and held it. Would she ever get used to the fact that he was hers?

———

RAFE STARED up at the beautiful creature on top of him with breasts worth paying homage to. Her skin glowed in the dim light of the room. With every glance from under her lashes and every tentative touch of her fingertips, his whole body felt like it was being stroked to full blaze. Vaguely he wondered if spontaneous combustion was a myth. Add in the euphoric feeling that surged through his blood every time she touched him, and he was likely to come in his jeans.

But was he going to stop her? Hell no. Her breasts swayed as she shifted her straddle farther down his legs. Her hands came into contact with the button on his jeans, and his cock throbbed and strained against the zipper. Involuntarily his hips rose, and he tried to school his breathing.

Since the hotel, he'd been terrified of the possibility of never seeing her again. He'd suddenly understood why they pulled agents off active duty if they got married. All he'd been able to think about was her.

The zzzpt sound of his zipper going down made Rafe wish he practiced some kind of Zen Buddhist religion. If he could find his center, he might have a chance of lasting long enough to make love to her. But it seemed Diana was in the mood to torture him.

Slim-fingered, delicate hands grabbed on to the top of his pants and boxers and tugged them down.

Scooting back, she pulled them down past his ankles, and he lay before her, naked as the day he was born. Diana's eyes traveled from his toes up his shins, to his thighs, and fixated on his dick.

His cock jerked as if to say hello. She shimmied back up his body, straddling him again at the knees. She supported her hands on either side of him.

"You're very big."

He grinned. "I love a woman who appreciates what she sees."

When she leaned directly over his straining cock, her long hair brushed against his skin, and her breath floated over the rigid length of him. It only took too puffs of breath from her, and his control snapped.

His hands banded around her biceps, and he hauled her up against him so he could kiss her. Flipping her onto her back, his hands flew to the waistband of her jeans, and he all but ripped off the button in an effort to get to her skin.

Yanking down the denim, he slid back up her body and wedged a knee between her thighs.

Against him, he could feel the moisture of her slick core through her panties. He tried not to think about how soft she was. He needed to go slow with her. His cock, on the other hand, had a mind of its own and pulsed against her thigh.

He gave her a peck on the lips before tracing feather-light kisses along her jaw. When he nuzzled her neck, Diana giggled. When he went from nuzzling to nibbling, she moaned. His hands enjoyed free rein of her breasts, testing the weight of the full globes, teasing the tight buds to pucker. Her hips rose to meet his every time he tugged on one of the rose-colored tips.

His lips continued a path down her ribs to her belly button. When the tip of his tongue dipped into the tiny crevice, she parted her thighs on an exhale.

Lifting his head, he watched her expression as he stroked her slick folds with his thumb. She widened her legs and transferred her hands to dig at the sheets. Gently circling the nub of her clitoris with his thumb, he eased one finger into her slick, dewy channel.

Immediately her muscles clenched around his finger, and a tingle started at the base of his spine. *Shit.* All he was doing was touching her, and he was already about to blow.

Slowly his finger retreated, then entered her again. When she exhaled, she whispered his name. The soft "Rafe" filled the silence in the room.

All he wanted was to hear her say it again. He slid his finger inside her again, followed by an achingly slow retreat, and she whispered, "Oh God."

Diana rotated her hips under his hands, coating his fingers with her juices. "Rafe, please—"

With her hips doing half the work, Rafe began moving his fingers again. Gently making love to her while his thumb stroked her clit. Her hips began to move in time with increasing tempo. She rode his fingers, and Rafe was mesmerized by her soft flesh. Gently he removed his fingers, ignoring the protest from her, and instead replaced them with his tongue.

Diana gasped and sat up in the bed, but he didn't stop, just held her legs wide, splaying her softness to him. While his thumbs parted her folds, he lapped at the sensitive flesh as she quivered around his tongue. The more he lapped at her, the wetter she became.

Rafe could tell the moment she gave in to the sensations. She lay back against the sheets and held his head in place while trying to widen her thighs. Tracing circles around her clit with his tongue, he drove her higher and higher until her whole body tensed.

Her inner walls quivered against his questing tongue, and her breathing came out in labored puffs. Placing a gentle kiss on the sensitive button, he drew himself back up her body, using his elbows as support. She blinked up at him with wide eyes. "You're very good at that, Mr. DeMarco."

"You sure do know how to stroke a guy's ego, don't you?" he drawled.

Diana reached between them, and her delicate fingers closed around the rigid length of him. His vision blurred, and that tingle started at the base of his spine again. He'd known it from the moment he first saw her—Diana was trouble.

"I'm pretty sure this isn't your ego."

He dropped his forehead to hers. "Jesus, Diana."

She pumped him again but this time brought his cock to her dewy center. Rafe hissed a breath and squeezed his eyes shut. Why did she feel so fucking good?

Diana's nails scored his back, and he groaned. "Fuck. Diana." He pushed in to the hilt, and she hissed beneath him. He tried not to move, to let her get accustomed to him and breathe for a minute. But that voice in his head wouldn't stop. *Rush. Take. Brand.* He withdrew by increments, and she hissed again.

Her breathing still ragged, she slowly smiled up at him. "Yes. Rafe, please don't stop."

That was all the invitation he needed. Withdrawing to the tip of his cock, he surged forward, keeping up that slow and steady tempo until she started to claw at his back. Her hips pumped against his, her velvet sheath swallowing the length of him.

The walls of her slick lining started to convulse against him once more. He knew what was coming now. "That's it, sweetheart, come for me." He kissed her deep, one hand tugging at the tip of her breast. The other reached between them, his thumb finding the dew-slick button and circling it.

Diana threw her head back, arching her back and giving him unfettered access to her breast. "Rafe!" She called his name on a breath as her body shook beneath him.

As she rode the wave, he continued to drive into her, longing to keep her ride going as long as he could. Wishing he could stay in that bubble of bliss forever.

"Goddamn, Diana, you are so beautiful."

"You make me feel beautiful."

Rafe canted his hips again. He needed to come. But her velvet walls still clung to him, gently milking him, still driving him insane.

Flipping her over onto her stomach, he glided a hand down her smooth back to her perfect round ass. God, her ass was a thing of beauty. Even though she was slender, it was high and carved to fit his palms.

He drew her limp body up onto her knees. Leaning into her, he whispered, "Hold on to the headboard."

She flicked him a cocked eyebrow over her shoulder, but she complied.

"That's a good girl. Now spread your knees for me." When she parted her legs, he bit back a groan. That angle gave him the world's most perfect view of her ass. Shifting behind her, he covered her body with his again. "Are you sore, baby?" As he asked, he inserted one finger in her still slick center, and she moaned.

"A... a little."

But that didn't stop her from moving her hips in time with his questing finger. When he added another finger, she sucked in a quick breath of air but then moaned as his fingers retreated.

"Rafe, please, I just need—"

He lined his cock up with her sweet opening and whispered as he slid home. "I know. I need you too."

From this angle, he knew he wouldn't last long. As he held her hips tight and rode her, she called his name. Leaning over her as their hips locked in rhythm, he played with her breasts, relishing their sweet response to his touch. Just by hovering over the sensitive skin of the full globes, her nipples puckered, inviting him to touch, to tease, to pinch.

He also couldn't resist playing with her ass as he stroked her. He filled both palms with her cheeks, molding them as he filled her.

She let her head hang between her braced shoulders as she pushed her hips back to meet his every stroke. "God, that feels, so—"

Rafe knew the instant she started to come again. Her pussy began to milk his cock, and she threw her head back. Digging his hand into her hair, he gave her ass a quick tap. On contact, she broke apart. Her whole body shook, and he could only hold on for the ride.

As she shattered around him, his vision started to gray at the edges. The tingle that had started in his spine felt more like someone had hooked him up to thousand-volt electrodes as he pumped inside her. So close to heaven.

And then Diana reached back for him, digging her hands in his hair. "Yes, Rafe. I love you."

As blinding light exploded his vision, his whole body erupted in electric bliss.

15

Even after their explosive lovemaking, Diana had a hard time falling asleep. The idea of ending the standoff with her brothers kept rattling around her brain. She didn't dare bring it up to Rafe because she knew he'd just freak out again. Not that she didn't understand why. He loved her. And she loved him back, which was why she was more determined than ever to end this thing.

The next day, Diana waited until she could get Noah alone. It wasn't easy to find an opportune moment when there were so many people coming and going in the penthouse all day.

Good thing she was patient. She'd learned those lessons after watching Rafe for so long. The penthouse was busy as they had a business to run. But she bided her time. Despite all that was happening in her sphere, Blake Security still had other clients to keep safe. So she waited until Rafe was busy in the living room with Oskar and she saw Noah walk into his office.

This was probably going to be her only chance, so she followed him and closed the door behind her quietly. The entire room was surrounded by glass. Damn it, why did everything have to be so open? If Rafe walked by and saw her in here, he'd want to know why. She dropped down into the chair in front of Noah's desk and then slid down so the top of her head wasn't visible. Noah looked up then, finally noticing her.

"Um, hi? You know you have feet like a cat? What are you doing?"

Diana chuckled. Despite his stern demeanor, he was actually not a bad guy. And Lord, he was funny with some of the things that would come out of his mouth. He'd been good to her, considering.

Anyone else would have thrown out the chick who'd brought nothing but destruction and mayhem to his home, but Noah had been very welcoming.

"Trying to make sure that Rafe doesn't see me."

Noah glanced around warily. "And why don't you want Rafe to see you?"

"Because he's not going to like that I'm here. Or

that I'm about to ask you to do something that he's against."

Noah rubbed his chin. "If he's against it, then I'm probably not going to like this either."

Ever since she'd found out about Oskar's plan, Diana knew that they had to make it happen. It was the only way to end things.

"I want to help draw my brothers out of hiding. They're too smart to fall for just anything, and even though we can wait for them to get sloppy, I don't want to wait that long. There's way too much chaos they could cause in the meantime. The only thing they want as much as the Jewel of the Sea is me. They don't like that I'm here because I have too much information that can be used against them. If they think they can recapture me, they'll try it."

"You're right. Rafe isn't going to like this. And neither do I." Noah's face was like stone as he watched her.

Diana looked away from his penetrating gaze. He saw too much, just like his wife. But she had to convince him this was the best way to end this nightmare because she wasn't sure how much longer she could live like this. She put a hand gently over her abdomen. Knowing that she had a little life growing in there only strengthened her resolve.

Her child deserved to be safe and have both parents around. If anything ever happened to Rafe because he was trying to protect her, she didn't know what she'd do. She could see it as clear as Noah sitting in front of her. If they didn't end this soon, Rafe would get hurt.

"I know you don't like it, but I think you'll help me anyway."

"Why is that? You're perfect for him, by the way. Only Rafe would find a woman who was just as relentless as he is."

Diana smiled at the comparison. "Relentless is how things get done. This is the only way that we can control things. I'd rather take a risk when we've planned for it, than to have my brothers come for me. If we're surprised, things won't end so well for us. What if Rafe gets hurt?" She closed her eyes and then used her trump card. "What if Lucia gets hurt? Or, God forbid, the baby. I can't live with myself if this goes badly and someone else pays the price. Can you?"

Noah's fingers tightened around the pen in his hand. "What exactly do you propose we do? Because as much as I want to end this, throwing an innocent woman to the wolves isn't something I'm willing to do."

She gave him a fierce smile. "First you should know I'm not that innocent. And they might be wolves, but I am meaner and will fight dirty. I have a family to protect now. If I pose as bait, they'll come for me. I'm sure of it. I can lead my brothers back to the loft. If we're ready for it, we can make sure no one gets caught in the crossfire."

Noah's eyes were intense as he listened, but she was happy to see that he *did* seem to be listening. He nodded along as she made her points and then thrust his hands through his hair.

"I don't like this at all, but I can't disagree with you. This is probably our best chance of keeping things contained. It's still a risk though. Your brothers are unpredictable at this point. What if they don't want to come back here and instead try to take you somewhere else? What if they want to fly you out of the country?"

Those were the same concerns that Diana had, but she couldn't show any weakness or Noah would call off the whole thing.

"I acknowledge the risks, but we can plan for all those scenarios. Which is infinitely better than sitting here and waiting for the other shoe to drop."

He watched her for a long time and then nodded once. Diana felt like she'd just gotten a royal seal of approval. They still had a lot of work to do, but this was a start.

"When should we do it?" she asked.

"The sooner the better. I'll get the guys to come up with a plan, and then we'll hopefully be ready to go within a day or two."

"Good. The sooner we get this over with the better." Not just because she wanted it to be over but because it was going to be really difficult to keep Rafe from finding out.

As if he'd read her mind, Noah sent her a frustrated look. "I only hope he doesn't take me out once and for all after this is done."

———

RAFE GRINNED at his niece as she crammed one of his fingers into her mouth. The grin quickly faded when the little scamp bit him. "No, Izzy. No biting Uncle Rafe."

Isabella scrunched up her face but seemed to calm down when she realized he wasn't taking his finger away,

"I can't believe how strong she is," he muttered when she clung possessively to his finger.

"Apparently, that's what's supposed to happen. Hope she didn't get you too bad."

"Nah, I'm tough. She's my niece, so I'm going to

give her whatever she wants. Besides it was only my finger."

"Yeah well, in my world it's a nipple. Now *that* hurts."

Rafe would rather not think about his sister's nipples. He suppressed a shudder and turned his gaze back to the chubby baby in his lap with the big gray eyes and dark curls. Jesus, she was cute. He still couldn't believe Lucia was a mother.

From the moment Lucia had come into the world, he'd been her protector and her biggest fan. Being ten years older than her had been strange. He'd never felt the usual competitiveness or annoyance that his friends felt with their siblings. She'd always seemed like she was so vulnerable, and he'd taken his role as big brother seriously. His father had drilled it into his head that it was his responsibility to watch over his sister, and he'd only renewed that vow after the death of their parents.

"I am so proud of you, Lulu. You're an amazing mom."

Lucia looked stunned at his words. Her lips trembled slightly. "You're going to make me cry. Not that it takes much these days. Everything causes the waterworks since I had Isabella."

"I figured that when I caught you crying over that cupcake the other day."

She laughed softly. "Well, it was a really good cupcake."

He kissed her forehead. "I'm serious though. For so long I didn't think this kind of happiness was in the cards for either of us. I didn't care so much about me, but it seemed so unfair for you to be punished for my sins."

Lucia put her hand over his. "Those days are over. Things are different now. I had no idea this kind of happiness was even real, but Noah has shown me that a forever love is possible. I want that for you too, and I'm so glad you've found Diana."

Rafe's instincts were to deny it. History had made him wary of claiming good things for fear that they'd be taken away. But Lucia was right; things were different now. And he wanted to tell everyone that Diana was his.

"I'm glad I found Diana too. When I think about how easily I could have missed meeting her, it scares the hell out of me."

"Fate had other plans for you, big brother. Just don't screw it up."

"Got it. Any other advice for me?"

"Nope. That's it. But don't worry, I'll let you know if I think of anything else."

Rafe chuckled. He had no doubt she would. Hopefully she'd have a long life of telling him and Noah what to do.

"That reminds me that I should go check on her. I don't want her to feel like I've abandoned her to those crazies out there."

Lucia smacked his arm playfully. "They're our crazies, and we love them. They're part of the family now."

Rafe thought of the assorted group of men that had become like family over the past year and a half. He'd never admit it out loud, but she was right. He'd do anything for those guys out there because they'd already proven their loyalty. He stood up and kissed the top of Isabella's head before handing her over reluctantly.

"You need anything?"

"No. Oh wait, ice cream. Yes. I need ice cream. And a glass of orange juice. I know it's weird, but it's something I started doing when I was pregnant."

Rafe wrinkled his nose. "You want to drink orange juice while eating ice cream... You know what? Never mind."

He walked toward the kitchen, shaking his head.

After getting her items, he'd leave her to eat without an audience. It would turn his stomach to see milk products and orange juice being consumed at the same time. But then again, he'd better get used to the weird combinations now that Diana was pregnant.

The living room was empty, so before going to the kitchen, he stuck his head in his room. Empty.

Oskar was in the kitchen, drinking from a bottle of water. "Hey, what's up?"

"Nothing. Just getting some stuff for Lucia. Have you seen Diana? I haven't seen her all afternoon."

Oskar shook his head, looking confused. "I thought she was with you."

Jonas walked by.

"Hey, Jonas. Have you seen Diana?"

The other man looked confused. "Noah said she was with you."

For reasons he couldn't begin to deconstruct, Rafe started sweating. It was illogical to assume that something bad had happened to Diana anytime they were apart. Going forward, they couldn't be together all the time, something he would have to get used to. But he had great instincts, and listening to them had saved his ass more than a few times. So although logic told him to stay calm, his instincts told him something was wrong.

"Let her know I'm looking for her if you see her," Rafe said out loud.

He made sure to keep his expression calm and even. There was no use alarming everyone if she was just taking a nap or getting something to eat. But instead of checking their room again, he headed straight for Noah's office. As soon as he cleared the doorway and saw Noah's face, he knew.

"You son of a bitch. What did you do?"

Noah didn't bother denying it, not that it would have done any good. They'd known each other too long for bullshit. He could tell with just one look that Noah had done something the other man was now regretting.

"She wanted to end it. I couldn't say no to that. It's been too hard worrying and wondering when they'll strike."

Rafe could feel his rage rising so fast and strong that he wasn't sure he'd survive it. For years he'd existed as simply a tool. A weapon. Weapons didn't have families or loved ones or homes. He'd gotten used to not having anything to call his own anymore, Lucia and Nonna long ago banished to the part of his mind that he considered buried. But now that he actually had something of his own, something to protect, the thought of it being taken away was unfathomable.

Simply put, Rafe wasn't sure he'd survive losing Diana. To lose her after having her love... he might as well lose his own life.

"I'm going to kill you, Noah. If she dies, you die."

Noah didn't look shocked by the threat, but then men like them understood vengeance. "She's protected. I promise you. I would never let her truly be in harm's way. She's just drawing them out."

Rafe could barely get his next words out. "And if things don't go according to plan?"

Noah's words were as grave as the expression on his face. "Then God help us all."

16

Diana was starting to reconsider the sanity of what she was doing. There she was in the middle of Central Park like a sitting duck. She knew she was being watched.

You've got this. You're armed. You've been trained. Maybe, but she knew just how far her brothers were willing to go. What if she miscalculated?

The plan was simple. Let them catch her. Not even try to run away. They would inevitably take her back to the penthouse where everyone was waiting. Matthias had installed a tracking chip in one of her sneakers. So if Hans and Jakob tried to take her anywhere else, the team would know.

The other good news was that Dylan was somewhere around here undercover. Whether he was the guy jogging in the baseball cap around the park or the other guy playing soccer with a bunch of kids over to her left, he was around here. If her brothers lost their damn minds and tried to kill her in public, he'd hopefully get to them first. She just prayed he was a hell of a shot.

As it turned out, she didn't have to wait too long. Within thirty minutes of when she sat on a park bench and tried to read a book and look somehow inconspicuous, Jakob sat right next to her. "We've missed you, little sister."

It was hard not to recoil at the sound of his voice. "Oh yeah? Is that why you were trying to kill me?"

Her brother sighed. "If I had it my way, we wouldn't have tried to kill you. But you know Hans. He has a temper. He just wanted you to give him what you found. Instead, you gave him a blank flash drive. That was very naughty."

"Well, I didn't know it was blank at the time." Diana turned to face her brother and studied his handsome features carefully. They were a more masculine version of her own. He had thicker brows, a stronger nose, and the same light eyes. How could they look so similar but be so different? How could he be a criminal? How could he be someone who hurt people for a living? For money?

"So, where's Hans? I know he's lurking around here somewhere."

He inclined his head toward the exit. "He's waiting for us. We're going on a little trip."

She shook her head. "I'm not going anywhere with you."

"Yes. You are."

It was then she noticed that his hand was in his jacket pocket. He had a weapon on her. What exactly, she couldn't be sure.

"What makes you think it's a good idea for me to go with you? Either way you're going to kill me. So why would I go peacefully?"

"We're not trying to kill you. We just want what's ours. That diamond. Uncle Boris is willing to buy it from us. That way we'll get out of debt with him and still have plenty to invest and grow the businesses Papa started."

"You call those businesses?" she spat. "You're trafficking young girls."

He shrugged. "Whores. They're a lucrative business. What else are we supposed to do?"

"If you just took those brains and applied them to something legitimate, imagine what you could do. Imagine how you could help people."

"You always were so naïve. You were always willing

to accept those princess dresses and your fancy boarding schools. How do you think those things got paid for?"

Diana stiffened her back. "You do know that mother was rich before she met Papa, right? You recognize that diamond was hers. The disdain you show for women is disdain you are showing for her."

"Mother, like all women"—Jakob scooted a little closer to her—"wasn't bright enough to see the big picture. That's why Papa couldn't trust her with what he was doing."

Diana just shook her head. "What happened to you? I remember you being bookish and loving to learn."

"Like you, I was naïve. Now get up. Otherwise, I will use this on one of the children."

He knew how to get her to go, and she stood easily. "I will not get in a car with you."

Her brother smirked. "Who said we're going in a car? I believe your penthouse apartment is somewhere near here, isn't it? You are staying with Rafael DeMarco, right? How does it feel to know that he's the one who killed Papa? And you let him put his hands on you."

Diana itched to slap him... or worse. She could

probably get a good kidney shot in before Hans killed her from wherever he was hiding. But she kept her feelings under control.

At the entrance to the park, Hans sat on a stone slab eating a hot dog. He grinned when he saw her. "Diana. You have given Jakob and I quite the fright. We are thrilled to see you again."

Diana struggled in Jakob's grip. She wanted to at least give the appearance of fighting them. If she made it too easy, they would know they were walking into a trap. "Whatever you two have planned, it's not going to work."

Hans leaned forward, and she smelled the sauerkraut and onions on his breath. "Oh we're going to get into that apartment. Because you're going to walk us right in."

Jakob shoved her forward, and she almost fell into Hans. With each of them flanking her, she walked along the path that would lead them to the main street, thinking of ways to delay the inevitable. *Make it look good, Diana, make it seem real.* Once along the path, she tried to run in the opposite direction. She hoped that didn't trigger Dylan to spring into action. But nothing happened.

She made it about half a block before Jakob

grabbed her around the waist. She kicked a little bit, but the idea was to eventually be caught.

When Jakob brought her back to Hans, her oldest brother tsked. "It is so disappointing that you tried to run, Larissa. If you act like that, I'm going to think you don't want to spend time with us."

"Wherever would you get that idea?" she muttered under her breath.

Hans chuckled. "Jakob, I think she's cross with us. You're the one who decided to become father's killer's whore." He patted her down and relieved her of her weapons, tsking softly.

Fuck, she was going to need those. "I am not a whore," she spat.

Hans shrugged. "You're sleeping with him. You're a whore. It's a shame you won't live through the night. We could easily bring you in on the family business. On the working side, of course."

Diana purposely struggled against his hold. What the hell was wrong with him? Why did they hate her so much? "Why are you so horrible? What have I ever done to you?"

Jakob scoffed. "For starters, Father was going to honor the deal with Boris. He planned to hand you over with the diamond when you were twenty-five."

Hans rolled his eyes. "The original plan was for us

to kill Boris and keep the diamond. Whatever happened to you after was of no consequence to us. But then we found out that you and the diamond were payment. That Boris had bought into the family business. After that revelation, we came up with the plan to kill him. He had squandered our future."

Diana froze with a gasp in her throat. "You had Papa killed?"

Hans chuckled. "Considering you're our sister, you are pretty stupid. Yes. We ordered the hit. We called a member of a black-ops team. He presented father as a threat to be taken out to his superiors. Given father's business practices, the US government sanctioned a hit on him. Best hit we ever called."

Diana couldn't believe it was her own brothers who wanted him out of the way so they could take over. To rob her of her birthright. Three more blocks to the penthouse. "You killed him?"

Hans laughed. "Plausible deniability, of course. But yes. Except Orion backstabbed us and stole the diamond for himself the night before the murder."

So Orion had absolutely taken it. And that had all been her brothers' doing. "I hate you."

Hans laughed, a belly laugh that made his whole body shake. "The feeling is mutual, little sister. I promise."

When they arrived at the penthouse, Diana struggled against Jakob's hold as he forced her hand on the pad for the handprint scan. And then they forced her face up to the retinal scan. Once they were inside the building, they shoved Diana toward the service elevator that led to the penthouse. She stumbled deliberately, praying that everyone was out of danger. Praying that they were all paying attention to where she was.

When the doors to the elevator opened, Diana took a deep breath and did exactly as she'd been instructed. She ducked while simultaneously delivering two groin strikes to her brothers.

Just as she scrambled out of the elevator, the lights went out. It was time to get to work.

———

DIANA'S HEARTBEAT was too loud in her head.

Boom. Boom. Boom.

She knew the plan. Crawl through the foyer. Make it into the kitchen. One of the guys would be in there, lying in wait. There was also someone in the living room and stationed in the hallway. There was also supposed to be someone posted in front of the panic room as a last line of defense. But there was a problem with that plan.

Her brothers were faster than she thought. Even though it was dark in the penthouse thanks to the blackout shutters, one of them had the wherewithal to reach out and snap a hand around her ankle. Diana screamed and thrashed and kicked. "Fuck you," she panted, the cries ripping out of her throat. *Focus. Calm down, you know how to get out of this. Think about your training.*

She forced her body over so that she lay on her back, then kicked her leg up and hooked it over the one her brother held. With the quick, sharp movement, he had to let go.

But then she heard gunshots whizzing over her head. All she could do was keep her head down. She knew Rafe and company had night vision. She knew JJ and Lucia were supposed to be safe in the panic room. She knew all those things, but it didn't help to quell her panic.

Crawl forward. One hand in front of the other. It didn't matter if her brother was trying to drag her back into the elevator to hold her hostage. She was going to make sure her new family was safe.

Where was Dylan? He should have come up the back stairs by now. All she had to do was stay down, stay safe, and not catch a bullet. But then from behind her, she heard a gunshot. Not like the guns Noah and Rafe had with their silencers.

There was no way she was going to make it crawling. She had to stand and run. *And risk getting hit.* It was worth the risk. Because she was not going to let her brother catch her.

Diana pushed herself to standing even though her bones protested. She knew the fate that awaited her if she didn't make it to safety. And she was so not down for that. She shoved herself up and ran, heading straight for the kitchen.

She heard the heavy footfalls behind her but just kept running. And then out of nowhere, someone came out of the side of the kitchen and shoved her out of the way. She tripped and sprawled forward. Fuck, she was done for. But nothing came. No one landed on her. No one was dragging her back by her hair.

She could still hear the sounds of footsteps, but there were too many of them. Had Noah called in more backup? Diana pushed herself to her hands and knees and twisted her head around. She needed to find some fucking weapons and quick. Thanks to the slivers of sunshine peeking in through the darkened shutters in the living room, her eyes adjusted to the darkness.

Someone had Hans. And it sounded like one hell

of a fight. The grunting, the cracking, the breaking of bones.

The elevator dinged again, but this time when it opened, there were more men. Where the hell had they come from? Diana counted at least four even in her haste to scramble away.

But then she couldn't move because Jakob was on her. He'd pounced on her, slamming her face into the marble. Pain exploded in her head. She tried desperately to remember what she'd learned in her krav maga classes as his hands locked around her neck. And then it came to her. She quickly brought her own hands up to her neck and sharply yanked his hands off her skin. And then she did the simplest thing in the world. She brought her knees to her elbows in one swift move. And her brother was off of her.

He fell forward but was on his feet in a moment. And coming for her. Diana attacked first, lunging right for him. She placed her thumbs over his eyelids and pushed. He screamed as his head went back, exposing his throat. She made a fist and delivered one swift jab to his Adam's apple. Jakob doubled over, choking and gasping for air. She grabbed his ears and brought her knee up to connect to his face. His head snapped back again, and he flailed. She took that opportunity to run.

The living room wasn't an option. She'd be trapped

in there, so she headed to the left toward Noah's office. He'd have weapons in there. With weapons she could fight better.

Even as she turned and prepared to fight whomever was coming, she saw that someone else had engaged with Jakob. The hand-to-hand was on. But her brother had a knife. "Be careful," she called out to Ryan.

Hans had been fighting Dylan. He'd come up through the back stairs only to find the melee in progress. The other men who'd come off the elevator were now engaging the members of Blake Security. Everywhere she turned, punches were being thrown and kicks were being landed.

Suddenly Ryan went down in a heap. He was bleeding from his side, and he wasn't moving. She didn't know what to do, and Hans was coming right for her.

She needed to get to Ryan, but she'd have to go around her brother first. It was one thing for her brothers to come after her. To hurt her. But there was no way she was going to let them get away with hurting her new family. She had to get to Ryan. Was he okay?

Diana used the palm of her hand to strike her brother right in the nose. He howled, but his head did not snap back. Instead, he looked angry and like he wanted to kill her. *Shit.* She had no choice but to run.

As she darted back into the kitchen, she grabbed whatever she could find. *The knives, yes.* She grabbed one then tossed it at her brother. She'd never done much knife training, just how to defend against them, not throw. Even as she ran toward the bedrooms in the gym area, she heard Hans curse behind her.

Then someone else was in the kitchen. She couldn't see who, but the shadows told her he was also big. That could be anyone, but when she looked closer, she realized it was Noah. And Jesus Christ, it was brutal. Hans was not playing around. He had the knife she'd thrown at him, and he'd already sliced through Noah's shirt. There was blood.

She had to distract him. She had to find a way to help Noah. *Something.* And then she saw the copper pans hanging over the sink. As quickly as she could, Diana ran and grabbed one of them and slid her grip around the handle.

She tiptoed behind them. Noah gave her a firm shake of the head, but she paid no attention. And with a wide arch of her arms, she cracked the copper pan on the back of her brother's skull. He went still. With his attention diverted for just one second, Noah delivered a blow to his kidney. Diana saw the knife too late. No, that wasn't a knife. "Oh my God, Noah, he's got a gun."

The shot rang out, and Noah went down.

Oh God. No, not Noah. Oh God. Logic dictated that someone would be on guard at the panic room. Maybe Matthias? Where was Rafe?

But then things went really wrong. The lights came back up, and she saw that everyone was engaged. There were far too many of them, and she'd led the enemy straight here. It was one thing to set a trap for her brothers, but the team hadn't been prepared for this.

Jonas was engaged in hand-to-hand combat as he fought someone in the kitchen, close to Noah's body. Oskar now engaged Hans. Matthias was fighting someone in black. Where was Rafe? A quick scan of the rooms and she found him by the gym.

The look on his face was brutal, deadly. He meant business. As the guy he was fighting went down, Rafe spared her a glance and mouthed the word, "Run."

And she was going to. She even turned around and headed straight for the panic room. But then she saw Jakob with his gun raised. A gunshot rang out, and Diana's insides turned to ice. No. Not Rafe.

Rafe froze in his tracks before staggering another couple of steps. Jakob fired another shot. This time

Rafe fell to the ground, even as he tried to fight. *What was happening?*

She was frozen, and shock rendered her unable to move. But she had to. This was her family, and she had to fight. Jakob fired another shot in her direction, and she ducked behind a pillar. Jonas elbowed the guy he was fighting in the temple. The guy went down. Jonas got him by the neck, then very calmly grabbed him by the top of the head and the chin and twisted.

Diana heard the crack, and her stomach roiled.

Matthias was shot but still fighting. When Diana peered back around the pillar, Jakob was on Rafe. He straddled him, raining fists on his face.

But Rafe was fighting off the blows. No. This was not how it ended. Her child was not going to grow up without a father because of who her family was.

She had zero fucks left to give. And she was not giving up on her man.

In the kitchen, Jonas had Hans pinned down. In the foyer, Dylan was starting to stir. And then there was Noah. Thank Jesus, Noah was moving.

He and Oskar were the only ones still engaged in hand-to-hand combat. He took a kick to the sternum and flew back, but he was up in an instant. He looked savage and raw and lethal. Even as beautiful as he was, that man was nothing but deadly. Nothing but a stone-cold killer.

Rafe was fighting for his life, and she ran straight for him. She didn't know where it came from, but a roar bubbled up deep inside and she screamed. Her brother looked up with a sneer. She didn't know where she gathered the strength, but she delivered a round-house kick so hard to his face he staggered back, then shook his head slightly as if trying to shake it off. While he was temporarily disoriented, Diana lunged.

Putting her full weight behind her body, she managed to push him back until he was off Rafe and on his back. She grabbed his ears and planted her thumbs in his eye sockets again.

She was not having it. She kept pressing as hard as she could. She was weak and tired, but she didn't dare let up.

Behind her, someone wrapped arms around her and picked her up as if she were nothing more than a doll. "Let me go. I will kill you."

"I'm glad to hear that, princess. But let me do this. You go to the panic room. Now."

"Rafe?"

"Yes." He put her down gently, and she turned in his arms.

"You're okay? But you were shot."

"I'm wearing a bulletproof vest. We all are. All except you. Now go. Let us deal with the rest of this."

Jakob groaned again. But this time Rafe just reached into his back holster, pulled out his gun, and fired a shot to his shoulder.

Diana didn't even flinch.

"Baby, panic room. Do not watch this. Do not see the thing that I am. Please go."

"I'm going but only because you need to stay safe and I distract you. But I'm not afraid of you. I see *all* of you, and I love you."

She turned to head for the panic room as she was told, but when she looked around, she could see that all the other men had their assailants either down or dead. Hans, unfortunately, was still alive. Though groaning.

"Looks like it's over."

Rafe pulled her close. "Still, go back to the panic room. We need to move the bodies out of here and call the cops. You don't want to be here for this. I'll come get you when it's time to make your statement."

"Okay, I'm going." But first she had to see. She lifted his shirt to see the thin fiber that might as well be vinyl for all she knew. Sure enough, there was a flattened bullet stuck to it. "Oh my God. Things like that exist?"

He nodded. "One day I'll show you all the tech I've got. But in the meantime, please, let me do this."

JJ came storming out of the back hallway. "So who do I call to move an unconscious body? Some guy tried to take Isabella, so Lucia kicked him in the nuts so hard he passed out. Also, I might have kept kicking him while he was down."

Noah grinned from his crouched position by the kitchen island and pushed to his feet. Jonas shook his head. "Baby, what have I told you? If the guy is down, you run. You don't keep kicking him."

She shrugged. "He tried to take my goddaughter."

Noah groaned. "What the hell were you doing out of the panic room anyway?"

JJ flushed. "Uh…"

Noah just rolled his eyes. "Lucia made you because she was worried about me?"

The pretty blonde folded her arms. "I plead the fifth. So which one of you burly men is going to come take out the trash? I'd do it, but I just did my nails."

Rafe turned his attention to the team. "Dylan, Ryan, call our cleanup guys to come and deal with the bodies. Jonas, Oskar, you call the feds. Get them in here for anybody who's still alive. Noah, you go deal with your wife and daughter. If I know my sister, she's guarding that body to make sure he doesn't get up again."

Diana watched him as he took full control of the room. This was the man she loved. And after today, she was going to get to keep him.

———

CLEANUP AFTER A SCENE like that would normally take days. But the crew that Noah had on call for emergencies took care of things pretty fast. The FBI would likely have some additional questions. After all, the story they'd given about how they'd apprehended Hans and Jakob Vandergraff was a little too pat to be believed. But in the end, they didn't have much of a choice.

Rafe had hand delivered them their targets on a silver platter. Even Interpol would rather have them than not. So he expected, once the bullshit final interviews were over, that they would be in the clear. The events of the past day would just become one more mission he locked away never to think or speak of again.

If only it would be that easy for Diana. Rafe's stomach flipped just thinking of it. His perfect warrior, Diana. He wished she wasn't made for this sort of thing, but he had to admit, she had been one hell of an asset.

Having to lie and keep secrets, all the while knowing that she was putting her own brothers away for life. With every hour, he'd watched as the light in her eyes dimmed a little bit more and wondered how much more she could take.

Rafe leaned forward and looked through the window of the boardroom as Diana gave her final statement to the FBI taskforce. He'd wanted to be in there to support her through it, but Granger wouldn't have it. He gritted his teeth. His old buddy just had to give him one last fuck you on the way out the door. But that was fine because after today, they were done.

They were finally free.

Emilie Durand stepped into the hallway first. When she spotted him, she straightened her shoulders. "I didn't think your little Diana would come through. I underestimated her."

"You underestimated both of us." Rafe had a hard time keeping the smile off his face at her disgruntled look. She sniffed and then walked away. Women like her weren't used to being denied, which made it all the more satisfying that Rafe would be the one she remembered as untouchable.

Ten minutes later, Alan left the room. When he

spotted Rafe standing outside waiting, a wry smile twisted his lips. "I had a feeling you wouldn't be far away."

"You know it. Is she free to go?"

Alan nodded. "You both are free to go."

They turned as Diana joined them in the hallway. She immediately gravitated toward Rafe, wrapping an arm around his waist. After her brothers' capture, there'd been a noticeable difference in the way she treated him. Not in the way Rafe had feared. He'd been worried that after seeing the terrible things he was willing to do that it would color her love for him. Not that he thought she'd leave him, he knew she was made of stronger stuff than that. But he worried that she'd always see violence when she looked at him. Or even worse, that underneath it all, she would fear him. He wasn't sure he could have survived if he'd looked in her eyes and known that she was afraid of him.

But instead, Diana had only drawn closer to him in the days since.

"So no more worrying about my crazy brothers? No one trying to kill us? What about Uncle Boris?"

Alan looked behind him to where Emilie stood. "With all the information the two of you have provided, Interpol has already built a hell of a case against Boris Klinkov. He's going away for a long time after this. You're free."

"Free?" Diana repeated, looking a little dazed. "I'm not even sure what that'll be like."

"Quiet probably. I've heard crossword puzzles help to pass the time." Alan looked between them with a calculating gleam in his eyes. "Although I have to say, you have a cool head under pressure, Ms. Vandergraff. If you ever want a career in the bureau, we could use someone with your attributes."

"Not a chance," Rafe growled.

"I didn't think so, but it was worth a try." Alan gave a mock salute before he left.

Diana shook her head as they watched him go. "Some nerve, huh? Besides, it's not like I actually did anything heroic. I just sat there and waited to be rescued really."

Incredulous, Rafe pulled back. "Nothing? Diana, you came to New York determined to infiltrate the lair of one of the most notorious assassins the world has ever seen and find lost treasure. That's pretty badass."

There were men all over the world who would shake in fear if he growled at them, but Diana only snorted in laughter.

"Notorious assassin, huh? Well, your ego is definitely still intact."

Rafe grinned. "Always. But what I said is true. What you did was dangerous and ill-advised and also pretty much a suicide mission."

"Hey, I thought you were supposed to be making me feel better," she grumbled before elbowing him in the side.

"Like I was saying, it was all those things, but it was also ballsy as hell. I don't care how you look at this, what you did was definitely not *nothing*."

They'd been walking leisurely toward the front doors, but before they got there, Diana pulled him to the side.

"Do you really think so? After all the crazy and exciting things you've done, I'm sure what I did was no big deal compared to that. In fact..."

He could tell that something was still bothering her, which wouldn't do. When they left this building, Rafe wanted them to have a truly fresh start.

"Just spit it out."

She rolled her eyes. "It's just that you've done all those amazing things. And I wonder if we go home and make a life together... well, won't that seem a little... boring?"

Rafe tipped back his head and laughed. "Boring? The woman who once seduced me and then kicked me in the balls? The woman who broke into my safe and stole a lifetime's worth of accumulated blackmail material? The woman who lured two of Interpol's most-wanted felons into a sting operation all while being pregnant? Not likely. Hell, you're almost as badass as Serena Williams."

Diana slipped her arm through his. "I'll take that. Because from here on out, it's going to be us against the world."

17

T hree months later...

THERE WAS a gentle comfort about the last few moments before executing an op. All was quiet and you could hear the sound of your own heartbeat. For a man like Rafe, it was often the only times he'd felt peace.

Until Diana, he thought. Then again, Diana had changed a lot of things in his life. Too many to enumerate.

Rafe glanced over at the man on his left. Noah was outfitted in black head to toe just like he was. He also wore an earpiece. Rafe patted the utility vest he wore, which carried everything from knives to tape to zip ties. For years it had been his standard uniform when working. Putting it on this evening before going out had felt like donning an old uniform that didn't really fit anymore.

"Just like old times, huh?"

Noah shook his head. "Better. Our comms weren't this good back in the day. Remember the ones we used to have? You'd get all that interference at the worst possible moments. Then it'd let out that high-pitched sound that was loud enough to pop your eardrum."

Rafe laughed at the memory. Even though ORUS had always had the best technology available, it was undoubtedly true that the tech they'd used ten years ago would seem like absolute shit now.

"Things have definitely changed. But I think it was an advantage. Agents in our time were forced to learn to adapt to less than optimal conditions. The guys coming out now, hell, they'd probably call a whole op off if their tech goes down."

Noah grunted in agreement. "Probably. They don't make agents like us anymore."

"Are you two going to start snogging, or are we here to steal some shit?" Matthias's voice came over the line, interrupting their conversation.

Rafe almost laughed. It was one of the few times

he'd ever heard the kid sound happy. But he couldn't deny that he had a point. Waxing nostalgic could wait until afterward. When they were safely on the plane back to the States.

He glanced over at Noah. "Is it just me, or is Scotland Yard over there having way too much fun with this? The young ones used to be scared of us."

"Don't worry about me, old man. I'm just trying to get this done. If we miss our window, we have to stay another day and I don't want to have to explain that. I'm not scared of you two but them..."

Noah made a face. He was probably imagining Lucia if he had to call and tell her that their trip had been delayed. Rafe couldn't make fun of him because he didn't particularly want to explain it to Diana either. His feisty kitten had claws when she didn't get her way, especially now that her pregnancy cravings had kicked in.

"He has a point. Let's do this."

They crept around the side of the building, following the route they'd mapped out on the plane ride to Argentina. He'd been here before of course with ORUS, but without the powerful organization to grease the right palms, it had been a lot trickier than expected to get the information they'd needed. But somehow Matthias had gotten the information, and they'd landed that afternoon with only a scant eight hours total to execute their op and get out without attracting any attention.

He heard a thump and then a soft "clear" in his left ear. Rafe waited two seconds per their plan and then walked the pathway leading to the back of the house. He stepped over the prone body of the man who'd been on patrol for the past hour. They'd observed him for quite some time to discover his usual routine. He wasn't the most observant to start with but also had a penchant for stopping for candy breaks. Almost too easy. With the night guard out of commission, he was free to climb the side of the house and enter through the bedroom window that had been left open for them.

A light flashed from the dark bushes up ahead, Noah signaling that all was clear. Rafe reached into his utility vest and pulled out the grappling hook he hadn't used since he'd rescued Diana. It made him smile to think of it. Who knew that his less-than-honorable skills would land him the woman of his dreams?

Less than sixty seconds later, he was up the side of the building and climbing through the window into a dark bedroom. His eyes adjusted to the light quickly. There was a huge four-poster bed to his left, which meant that the safe was to the right. Exactly as he'd expected.

Rafe crossed the room quickly but quietly. It would have been so much better if they could have done this when the house was empty, but luckily, the home-owner was out for the night. The only people left in the house were staff, one of whom was responsible for helping them get in. He chuckled. Unhappy staff members were the worst security risk in the world. All they needed was a little money, and they were happy to see their employers fall.

In this case, they hadn't even had to offer that much money to convince the elderly valet to not only leave the window open for them but to plant a hidden camera.

"All good?" Noah's voice was quiet in his ear.

Instead of speaking and possibly giving away his position to any staff members walking in the hallway, Rafe tapped his earpiece three times, their code for *I'm busy, fuck off*. He could hear Noah's soft chuckle in response.

Rafe removed the painting from the wall that concealed the safe. It was one of those high-tech, digital safes. They could have used some advanced technology to crack the safe, but honestly it was just easier to watch the video footage and wait until the owner entered the code.

Maybe the younger agents aren't the only ones who are spoiled, Rafe thought wryly.

These days the challenge of an op wasn't what drove him anymore. Getting home safely to his fiancée was what mattered the most.

He entered the code and then stepped back as the door swung open. He ignored the stacks of cash and reached all the way to the back to grab a black fabric pouch. With one tug the drawstring loosened, and Rafe smiled down at his palm.

"Hello, beautiful."

———

DIANA WAS DREAMING.

She was conscious that it was a dream the whole time, but strangely it didn't bother her to know that. In the dream she was pushing a grocery cart. Pushing a grocery cart was actually a strange thing for her to dream about since she hadn't done it too many times. Growing up, her father's staff had done all that. She hadn't gone to a grocery until she was in college. But she was happily pushing a cart and checking items off a list. In the front of the cart, happily chewing on its fist, was a baby.

Her baby.

She smiled at the cherub-cheeked toddler and passed a hand over his short, dark curls. His brown eyes were bright and watchful as she grabbed a few things off the shelf and put them in the cart. It was such an ordinary scene, a mom shopping with her little boy in tow, but it hit Diana with all the force of a battering ram. This simple, everyday domestic scene represented the most secret longing of her heart. To have a family of her own that she could love and care for. There was only one thing missing.

Strong arms encircled her from behind, and she sighed into the embrace. The little boy let out a squeal at the sight of his daddy that brought a deep, rumbling chuckle from the man.

Diana loved that laugh and that she was one of the only people who could coax it out of him. He was her husband and the love of her life. She'd never felt safer or happier than she did right then.

"I love you, Rafe."

His answer was a soft kiss to the side of her neck.

"Diana. Wake up, sweetheart," he whispered.

After a few moments, Diana opened her eyes and

blinked as the dream faded away. She'd come into the room for a nap right after lunch and meant to wake up after an hour. Rafe, Noah, and Matthias had been out of town on a quick business trip overnight, and the place had seemed so quiet and boring without them. She knew Lucia felt the same way even though JJ had been working hard to take her mind off Noah's absence. Diana had been counting down the hours until they were expected back. She suspected that everyone else was too. Having one cranky, lonely pregnant chick, with a worried wife and toddler in residence couldn't be fun for the others either.

The light in the room indicated that she'd slept much later than she'd intended. At a soft brush against her cheek, she turned her head. Rafe knelt beside the bed, watching her with a gentle look on his face. It shouldn't have been such a surprise; she'd been expecting him home in the early evening. But it still took her off guard how happy just the sight of his face could make her.

"You're home!" She sat up and threw her arms around his neck. Laughing, he caught her to keep them both from tumbling to the floor.

"Careful. You've got precious cargo on board." He rested a hand on the curve of her belly. His thumb traced a gentle path back and forth. *Gently. Reverently.*

She was barely showing at four months, but if you

were looking, you could definitely tell she was pregnant. Diana thrilled with every new change in her body because it was evidence of the amazing little person she and Rafe had created.

Together.

"I was so tired that I wanted to take a nap before you were due home. But I must have slept longer than I meant to."

He kissed her forehead softly. "Is my daughter wearing you out?"

She grinned. They'd had a running feud for the past month about the sex of the baby. Neither of them wanted to find out beforehand, happy to leave it as a surprise. Rafe, however, was convinced it was a girl. Mainly because he said the universe loved to challenge him.

"Our *son* is doing just fine. I was craving sauerkraut yesterday, but I managed to survive it."

She cringed just thinking of it. Jonas had been a great sport and gone out to buy her some. It had been delicious while she was eating it, but thinking back on it made her gag a little. It was so strange how she could crave things so intensely and then as soon as she had them, revert back to thinking they were gross.

"Do I owe the guys a favor? You didn't make them watch you eat ice cream and pickles, did you?"

"That is a stereotype. I have never eaten anything weird with my ice cream." Diana *had* eaten the sauerkraut and then eaten a cherry Popsicle right afterward, but he didn't need to know that.

When she tried to stand, Rafe put a hand up to keep her from rising. Before she could ask what he was doing, he reached into his pocket and pulled out something that she couldn't see. Her heart started beating wildly for some reason, but she wasn't sure why. Diana just had a sudden feeling that Rafe was up to something.

Then Rafe opened his hand.

Diana put a hand over her heart. "Is that... is that really..."

"The Jewel of the Sea," Rafe finished for her. "Yes, it is. I thought long and hard about what I could possibly buy for you that would express my feelings. Diamonds are traditional, of course, but you and I have never been the traditional sorts. Starting our lives together shouldn't be traditional either. So when I give you a gift, I need it to be something more. Something meaningful."

"So you found my mother's stone for me?" Diana almost couldn't speak over the lump in her throat.

She'd long ago reconciled herself to the reality that the Jewel of the Sea was lost forever. It had been stolen, sold, and likely crossed many paths on the black market since. Something that valuable wasn't going to be easy to find. Then she'd found peace with it. Her connection to the stone had nothing to do with its value but its legacy. Her fingers trembled as she reached out and touched the cool surface of the jewel.

This was the only thing she had left of her mother.

The authorities had seized her family estate in Austria, and they'd gotten word that it had been looted shortly after that. Probably payback from her brothers' many enemies. It made her sad to think of her mother's things being carted off by criminals, but again, she'd made peace with it. She'd had no plans to go back there anyway.

Her life was here now. Her life was Rafe now.

"Do I even want to know what you had to do to get this back?"

Rafe suddenly looked cautious. "Probably not. But I wanted you to have it because it was your mother's."

Diana would never stop marveling at his kindness. If asked to describe himself, Rafe would undoubtedly use words like *stoic, determined,* and *relentless.* But Diana saw an entirely different side to him. She saw attentiveness and a sweetness that should have been impossible in someone who'd been through the things he had. Quite simply, he'd shown her what it was like to be loved unconditionally and completely.

She pulled him in for a soft kiss before turning her attention to the stone in his hand.

"I never expected to see this again. My mother told me when I was a little girl that the Jewel of the Sea had been handed down from mother to daughter for more than ten generations. It's supposed to carry good fortune. Not that it worked for my mother." She smiled sadly.

"Well, you don't need it for good fortune, but I figured this was as good an engagement gift as any."

Her eyes shot wide open when she realized what was happening. They'd discussed marriage of course, but Rafe had always talked like it was a done deal. She hadn't expected to get a proposal.

"I love you."

Her eyes watered at the heartfelt declaration. "I love you too."

"Which is still a revelation to me." Rafe laughed. "From the moment I saw you looking all dirty and defiant, I knew that my life would never be the same. Happiness wasn't something I thought was possible for me. But somehow that's what you do. You make me happy. I want us to always be together, getting in and out of trouble and fighting our demons together.

There's nothing in this world that I want more. Larissa Diana Vandergraff, will you marry me?"

The words were barely out of his mouth before she was screaming, "Yes!"

Laughing, Rafe wiped the tears from her cheeks. "Thank God. This jewel really is lucky. I just got the most beautiful woman in the world to agree to be my wife. I'll get you a real ring later, but I figured I'd better bring my A-game to this proposal."

"You didn't need any help. Just you." She closed her eyes. "I'm so excited for all this. Our whole lives."

"Me too. Because I can't do this without you," Rafe said.

"You'll never have to. I'm in too deep to get out now, Rafael DeMarco."

Which was exactly where she wanted to be.

———

THANK YOU for reading the DEEP duet. The next book in the Shameless Universe is about Matthias! It will release on 5/22/18. PREORDER at malonesquared.com

While you're waiting, catch up on Jonas and JJ's hilarious antics in their steamy, suspenseful novel - *FORCE.*

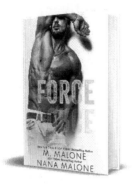

EXCERPT OF FORCE © August 2017 M. Malone and Nana Malone

JESSICA JONES CLOSED HER EYES, exhausted. Day after draining day of pulling double duty while her bestie and partner in crime was on maternity leave was starting to take its toll. Like hell was she going to start complaining, though. If anyone deserved happiness, it was Lucia. Her best friend had been to hell and back and deserved the time off.

JJ could deal. After all Lucia would do it for her. Besides, JJ wasn't letting a prima donna fashion designer run her into the ground and call uncle. She'd rather burn her Jimmy Choos first. She could handle anything their boss Adriana could dish out.

It felt like she'd only shut her eyes for mere seconds before she frowned in her sleep.

Something was wrong. *Very* wrong.

When she peeled her eyes open again, she was in hell.

"Oh my god," she screamed.

But that scream was her first mistake. It meant emptying out her lungs, which meant she needed to breathe... and that meant lungs full of smoke.

It was so hot her hair plastered against her head and her sheets clung to her naked breasts from sweat. Yeah, she slept topless, so what? It had been so hot lately.

Frantic, she looked around the room trying to find the source of heat. It was so dark she couldn't see anything. But she could feel the smoke all around her, cloying and thick, wrapping around her and constricting her lungs.

"Don't panic." The sound of her own voice out loud scared her out of her frozen state. *Fear immobilizes. Anger motivates.* That's right, get pissed off!

286 | M. MALONE & NANA MALONE

If there was anything JJ was good at, it was being hot tempered. What the fuck was smoke doing in her room anyway? She'd just had a goddamned blowout. She needed to charge that color and cut to whatever or whoever was the source of this fire.

Move your ass girly.

She had to move because she was *not* dying in this room. She did not survive her past to die like this. Fuck that noise. Besides, if she died like this, Lucia would resurrect her ass and kill her all over again. After Lucia had survived being stalked and almost killed, JJ had a new appreciation for the meaning of life.

She swung her legs over the side of the bed, letting out a sigh of relief when her toes met the carpet. Now that her eyes had adjusted to the dark somewhat, she could see the faint hint of an orange glow from down the hall. Which meant the fire hadn't reached her room... yet.

But the bedroom door stood open to the hall, which was probably why she could already smell the smoke.

It was weird that the door was open. She always closed the door before going to sleep. It was one of the things Lucia's husband had drilled into her. Noah owned a security company, and his overprotectiveness toward Lucia had spilled over onto JJ. Now she always had one of the annoying, albeit sexy, guys who worked for him trailing her to and from work, and her apartment had been subjected to a thorough security 'review' by Noah's resident IT wizard. Matthias had deemed her place 'merely acceptable.'

JJ was pretty sure they'd have asked her to move if they hadn't known from experience that she didn't take suggestions well. The last thing she needed was some man trying to tell her what to do. Maybe Lucia was okay with that, but she wasn't interested. JJ knew from experience that she didn't want any man having control over her life. Never again. That alpha-asshole shit didn't work for her, so they could shove their over protectiveness where the sun didn't shine.

With a quick glance at the open door, she realized it was actually lucky she'd left it open, otherwise she might not have woken up until the flames were closer. What the hell had woken her? *You can think through that shit after you're safe.* Yeah, good point. She grabbed up her comforter and wrapped herself in the thick fabric, bringing it up over her head as she stepped into a pair of slippers.

How far to the door? The window might be an option if the fire escape hadn't been welded over some years ago. She looked up and then squinted in the darkness. And then she saw the shadow in the hall. The man-sized shadow.

Fuck me. She opened her mouth to scream then reached into her bedside drawer for the nearest weapon she could find. She'd been aiming for the retractable baton she kept in the top drawer. But instead she'd come up with a gag gift from a bachelorette party a couple of years ago. A giant purple vibrator.

What are you gonna do with that? Fuck him to death? Well that was a thought.

"Who the hell are you? And what the fuck are you doing in my apartment?"

He stepped forward slightly, his body still half-hidden outside the door, and JJ raised her makeshift weapon.

"I'm here for you, Jessica. I'm always here for you."

JJ clutched the blanket closer, and her fingers curled around the vibrator as his voice washed over her. The low tone of his words sliced through her veins. That voice. It had been so long since she'd heard that voice. She'd hoped to never hear it again, except in her nightmares.

"How did you find me?"

His chuckle was almost as terrifying as the words that followed. "I never lost you."

JJ screamed and backed up so fast that she stumbled and fell on the bed. The comforter tangled around her and she fought against it, certain the next touch she'd feel would be the last.

Strong hands wrapped around her flailing arms.

"Damn it, you crazy woman, I'm trying to help you!"

It took a few seconds before she recognized the voice, her terror distorting it into the one she feared most. When she finally spoke, her voice was tiny.

"Jonas? Is that you?"

The comforter was pulled back away from her eyes, and Jonas's handsome face appeared. Jonas Castillo worked for Noah's security company and was a regular fixture in her life. He was routinely assigned to protect Lucia, and by default JJ, during the workweek. She took great pleasure in giving him hell, and he was usually cursing her name or bickering with her.

"Yes, of course it's me."

Before she could question what he was doing there, she felt herself being lifted. She clutched his shoulders automatically, disoriented after her fall. Now she wasn't sure if that had actually happened. Had she been dreaming? It was so hard to tell.

"Jonas, did you see anyone else in the apartment?"

"Like who? Don't you live alone?"

Was that jealousy in his voice? Even under these circumstances, JJ couldn't resist the urge to screw with him a little.

"Actually I don't. We can't leave without my favorite guy."

"Who? And if you have a boyfriend, where is he? Some help he is during an emergency."

"Well, Fluffy has never been much help during emergencies, but he blows the best wet kisses."

Jonas didn't pause. "I'll come back for your dog, I promise. But I have to get you to safety."

It must have been the smoke affecting her brain, because at first JJ didn't realize what he'd said. It wasn't until they were at the front door that she understood he meant to leave.

"No! I have to get Fluffy!" JJ swatted at his massive chest. She must have surprised him because his arms loosened around her legs, giving her the room she needed to jump down.

"Damn it, JJ! This is serious. We don't have time to stop."

"It'll just take a second." JJ raced back to the guest bedroom and grabbed Fluffy, covering him with the comforter as she ran.

Jonas picked her up as soon as she hit the hallway and ran for the front door. They passed a crew of firefighters in the corridor outside her apartment. The smoke was thicker out here, so JJ buried her face in Jonas's shoulder, making sure to keep Fluffy covered too.

When they got outside, Jonas set them down carefully on the grass, safely away from the building. An EMT approached, and Jonas pointed at JJ. She was going to protest, but dissolved into a coughing fit as soon as she opened her mouth. The young man frowned and knelt on the grass next to her. Then his eyes widened when her comforter slipped and she almost flashed an entire boob at him.

"Hey, eyes up, kid." Jonas glared at him before yanking his shirt off. He put it over JJ's head, and she maneuvered carefully to get her arms in without dropping the comforter completely. If she hadn't felt so crappy, she'd have told him exactly where he could shove it. She didn't need anyone speaking for her.

Just to annoy him, she gave the EMT a bright smile that had the young man blushing furiously. Jonas scowled at both of them.

After a flurry of activity, blood pressure cuffs, and oxygen, they finally left her alone. That's when Jonas got a good look at her again. Her *and* Fluffy.

"A fish? You risked your life to save a fucking fish?"

JJ scooped up Fluffy's bowl protectively. "Fluffy is

not just a fish. He's a Japanese fighting fish. A total badass."

Jonas looked like he wanted to strangle her. Normally that was exactly the effect she was going for, but strangely, it wasn't as satisfying as usual.

"Thank you, Jonas. For coming in after me."

He looked as shocked as she felt by her sudden gratitude.

"Of course. It's nothing. The fire department would have gotten to you soon. I just happened to get there first when Matthias said your alarms were triggered."

The talk of alarms brought back memories of the man she'd seen in the smoke. It had happened so fast, and she couldn't be sure what was real and what had been a dream.

"Did you see anyone in there?" At his confused look, JJ clarified, "In my apartment?"

Jonas knelt and looked her in the eye. "Was there someone in there with you, Jessica?"

It was all such a blur, and she didn't like the way he was looking at her. Noah's entire crew was extremely overprotective, so if she said the wrong thing, she'd end up on house arrest with Jonas as her jailor. Plus, it was likely it had all been a dream. Jonas had been in her apartment. He would have seen if anyone else was there. The man in the smoke was nothing more than a shadow from a past she'd rather forget.

"No, I meant in the building. I just want to make sure all my neighbors got out okay."

Jonas looked like he wanted to say something else, but Noah arrived just then with Lucia right behind him.

JJ accepted a hug from her friend, and that was when it really hit her.

"I guess I'm homeless now."

Noah's voice carried from behind Lucia. "You'll stay with us, of course."

JJ's eyes met Jonas's, and she knew he was thinking about her earlier question.

"It's for the best," Jonas said.

She glanced over at Lucia. "Free rent and a house full of hot men. Count me in."

ABOUT THE AUTHORS

NYT & USA Today Bestselling author **M. MALONE** lives in the Washington, D.C. metro area with her three favorite guys: her husband and their two sons. She holds a Master's degree in Business from a prestigious college that would no doubt be scandalized at how she's using her expensive education.

Independently published, she has sold more than 1/2 million ebooks in her two series THE ALEXANDERS and BLUE-COLLAR BILLIONAIRES. Since starting her indie journey in 2011 with the runaway bestselling novella "Teasing Trent", her work has appeared on the New York Times and USA Today bestseller lists more than a dozen times. She's now a full-time writer and spends 99.8% of her time in her pajamas. **minxmalone.com**

USA Today Bestselling Author, **NANA MALONE**'s love of all things romance and adventure started with a tattered romantic suspense she borrowed from her cousin on a sultry summer afternoon in Ghana at a precocious thirteen. She's been in love with kick butt heroines ever since.

With her overactive imagination, and channeling her inner Buffy, it was only a matter a time before she started creating her own characters. Waiting for her chance at a job as a ninja assassin, Nana, meantime works out her drama, passion and sass with fictional characters every bit as sassy and kick butt as she thinks she is. **nanamaloneromance.net**

Made in the USA
Lexington, KY
03 February 2018